AGATHA CHRISTIE

Mistress of Mystery

$\mathscr{A}$GATHA $\mathscr{C}$HRISTIE

MISTRESS OF MYSTERY

By G. C. Ramsey

Illustrated with photographs

DODD, MEAD & COMPANY

NEW YORK

Library of Congress Catalog Card Number: 67-19230

Printed in the United States of America
by The Cornwall Press, Inc., Cornwall, N. Y.

For Ellen Virginia Warnock
for whom Teaching is the Joy of Life

Acknowledgements

The most pleasant part of an author's work is the acknowledgement of the debt he owes the many people who help a book along from inspiration to publication. One of the author's great surprises was the willingness and even eagerness of mystery authors and critics to help with this project in any way they could. A forty-five-year literary career accumulates a great deal of facts, figures, publicity data, and lists which require thorough and repeated sifting and checking. Any faults which follow are solely the author's. But for the help of the following people, there would be a great many more.

Miss Nora Blackborow, executive secretary of Hughes Massie Limited, of London, who has the patience of Job and the efficiency of Miss Lemon.

Mr. Anthony Boucher, *The New York Times* mystery critic, who made many valuable suggestions.

Mrs. Aileen Eads Childs, the author's grandmother, who cheerfully read proof far into the night.

Mr. William Collins, the English publisher of the works of Agatha Christie.

Mr. Edmund Cork, head of Hughes Massie, London, who was kind and patient far above and beyond any call of duty.

Mr. Frederick Cowan, who typed the reference material.

Mr. Howard Haycraft, who has combined wit and scholarship, much to the credit of the detective story, and much to the help of its would-be scholars.

Mr. S. Phelps Platt, President of Dodd, Mead, who has given this project his wholehearted assistance.

Mr. Raymond T. Bond of Dodd, Mead, editor of Aggatha Christie's long-time publisher in America.

Mr. Peter Saunders, producer of the Christie plays, who answered innumerable questions.

Contents

x   Contents

Illustrations

AGATHA CHRISTIE

Mistress of Mystery

The 1948 Walter Bird portrait of Agatha Christie which is generally used for publicity purposes in connexion with her novels, plays, and movies.

Agatha Christie at the typewriter in her home, Greenway House, Churston Ferrers, South Devonshire, England. She types, she says "with three fingers of each hand, unlike most amateur typists, who only use two."

Mr. and Mrs. Max E. L. Mallowan on the grounds of Greenway House.

At the piano in Greenway House. Mrs. Christie was taught to play the piano and mandolin, and was sent to Paris in her teens to study singing. Elgar and Bach seem to be among her favourite composers.

Mrs. Mallowan's interest in interior decorating led to her owning eight houses at one time. Now she divides her time between Greenway House (shown here), their house near Oxford, and a flat in Chelsea in London.

Professor and Mrs. Mallowan off to a dig in Iraq, in January of 1950.

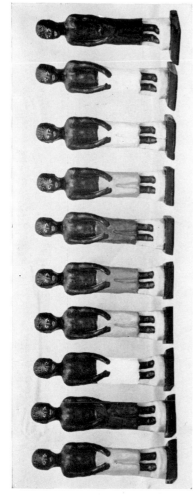

Closeups of the figures used in the stage productions of "Ten Little Niggers."

The Ten Little Ethiopian figures used in British productions. Made of moulded rubber, each with differently coloured pants. 9½" high. (From the author's collection.)

The Ten Little Indians used in American productions. Moulded rubber, with woollen blankets. 6½" high. (Reproduced by permission of Theatre Production Service.)

John Vickers

The stage set of "Ten Little Niggers," as it appeared in the original production, St. James's Theatre, London, 1944. Note the nursery rhyme on the wall to the left, and, below it, the ten figures.

The stage set of "The Mousetrap." In 15 years, the cast has worn out two sets of furniture.

This portait of Hercule Poirot was painted in the mid-1920's by W. Smithson Broadhead, on commission by *The Weekly Sketch,* who were then publishing the short stories later collected in *Poirot Investigates.*

Charles Laughton, as Sir Wilfred Robarts, confronts Marlene Dietrich in the 1956 film version of "Witness for the Prosecution." Laughton also played Hercule Poirot in "Alibi," Agatha Christie's first play, in 1928, at the Prince of Wales' Theatre, London.

Margaret Rutherford, as Miss Marple, conferring with her sidekick Mr. Stringer, in the film "Murder Most Foul." "Mr. Stringer's" real name is Stringer Davis, and in private life, Margaret Rutherford is Mrs. Stringer Davis.

At the telephone.

With her daughter, Rosalind : Agatha Christie, the great detective-story writer.

At her writing table.

At work with her type-writer.

In her drawing-room : the author of the series of detective stories we begin this week.

With "Tutankhamen cushions : Agatha Christie and her little girl.

CREATOR OF THE MOST INTERESTING DETECTIVE SINCE SHERLOCK HOLMES : AGATHA CHRISTIE.

Illustrated London News and Sketch, Ltd.

Agatha Christie and her daughter Rosalind in the early 1920's. This set was taken by *The Weekly Sketch* to illustrate the Poirot stories later collected in the volume *Poirot Investigates.*

AGATHA CHRISTIE

魔 術 の 殺 人

THEY DO IT WITH MIRRORS

アガサ・クリスティー

田 村 隆 一 訳

A HAYKAAWA
POCKET MYSTERY BOOK

Drawing by Helen Hokinson; © 1949 The New Yorker Magazine, Inc.

*"What I like about Agatha Christie is she's so full of surprises.
This time, she puts poison in cocoa."*

Above: A cartoonist's comment on Mrs. Christie's popularity.
Mrs. Christie was amused, but confesses that she can't remember ever putting poison in cocoa . . .

Opposite: The Japanese edition of *They Do It with Mirrors.* A
statistical survey published in England in the early 1960's showed
that Agatha Christie was England's second most-translated author. The first was Shakespeare.

Photo by staff photographer Paul A. Doherty, Boston Herald Traveler Corp.

Mr. and Mrs. Max E. L. Mallowan snapped in Boston in October 1966 during his United States lecture tour on his book *Nimrud and Its Remains*. This photograph accompanied an article in the *Boston Herald* on their two careers, entitled "A Houseful of Fame."

CHAPTER ONE

The Mystery Story as a Form

AS YET, very little scholarship has been done on the detective story as a literary form. First of all, the form is still relatively new, if one accepts the 1841 publication of "The Murders in the Rue Morgue" as marking the birth of the detective story, and this date is now generally so accepted. Thus, the detective story is a good century younger than the novel, if we take Henry Fielding's *Tom Jones* and other works to represent the birth of the novel, although, in point of fact, *Tom Jones* is rather more a group of loosely-knit adventures or short stories than a novel as we think of the term novel in the works of Thackeray, Dostoyevsky, or later writers. Scholarship in the field of the novel is really a twentieth-century development, and perhaps scholarship in the field of the detective story will be a product of the twenty-first, as it always seems to take time for scholars to catch up with what interests the common man, and still more time for them to persuade themselves that what the common man enjoys may possibly have intellectual merit and worth. We Anglo-Saxons remain rather Puritan about our literature, music, and art, and seem to feel that all three should improve us rather than merely amuse us. This present work will not attempt to argue that question, but we may note in passing that it is the taste of the general public (guided, we hope, by those of us who have chosen to spend our lives in the pursuit of intellectual things) which will in the end determine what works of literature, music, and art survive the test of time, and which ones will fall by the wayside.

Critics of the detective story as a form are quick to point out that the form has limitations. Edmund Wilson has called the characters two-dimensional, and he has a point. In a novel, the reader is expected to identify himself with one or more characters as they struggle through the pages of the book. He is expected to share Hamlet's tortured indecision, and perhaps find a parallel in his own life. Apparently Shakespeare was successful in creating a character with whom people could identify, and for whom they could feel sympathy, for the play has remained popular for hundreds of years, as have many good novels. Yet in the detective story or novel, everyone is to be considered a suspect and is to be highly mistrusted. As we do not like to consider our friends potential thieves and murderers, and few of us fancy ourselves in those roles, it is difficult if not impossible to have a detective story in which the reader can identify with any of the characters, and please remember that the detective and narrator are suspect, too.

Yet although the detective story will never give us a character of the calibre of Hamlet, perhaps the glory of the form is that it has presented us with so many Becky Sharps. In other words, detective writers have realised effectively the potential for caricaturing types, after the fashion of Charles Dickens or Richard Brinsley Sheridan. We do not identify with these characters or caricatures, yet we realise that we have met them, or people very much like them, and thus are able to believe in the action of the detective novel. For example, consider the departure of Katherine Grey from St. Mary Mead, in Agatha Christie's *The Mystery of the Blue Train*. Perhaps to the surprise of the Christie fan, it is not Miss Marple that we are about to present, but rather

> The little maid of all work, Alice, who brought a stiff wired nosegay and cried openly. "There ain't a many like her," sobbed Alice when the train had finally departed. "I'm sure that when Charlie went back on me with that girl from the Dairy, nobody could have been kinder than Miss Grey was, and though particular about the brasses and the dust, she was always one to notice when you'd give a thing an extra rub. Cut myself in little pieces for her, I would any day. A real lady, that's what I call her."

In very few words, we have been skilfully presented with a rather complete portrait of Alice, the epitome of kind, unintelligent faithfulness.

These minor characters, so skilfully drawn, pale beside the principals known from their spin-offs and their series. Perhaps the most famous caricature of all time is Sherlock Holmes, so vividly created by Conan Doyle, but he is presumably being given a run for his money in that never-never and ever-ever land of literature by Hercule Poirot, who, if he were sixty-five in 1904, is now by a conservative estimate at least one hundred twenty-eight. However, he seems to grow younger as he travels through the years—perhaps it is his hairwash that tints without dyeing. Hercule Poirot, and Miss Marple, together with the Beresfords, Enderbys, Clitherings, Battles, and others, appear and reappear in Mrs. Christie's novels, give letters of introduction to each other, have children, grow older (in some cases) and, in fact, behave strangely like people in real life except for one thing: they are completely unruffled by the excitement of murder. In a peculiar sense, the reader identifies with one or more of these characters because he has met them so many times before, or because he knows their friends. It would seem, therefore, that the inherent problems of characterisation can be got round by the skilful use of caricature and by the repetition of major and minor characters from one book to another.

Thus it would seem pedantic and short-sighted to condemn detective fiction out of hand because it is light and popular and must rely on caricature. Any form which seems to fascinate so many readers deserves scholarly attention.

This is not to say that popular demand does not result in the creation of a great many second- and third-rate examples of the form—it certainly does.

Yet this sad commercial fact ought not to keep us from considering first of all, what the detective story is, and secondly, what points it has in its favour as a form.

Howard Haycraft, whose excellent book *Murder for Pleasure* was written in 1941 to celebrate the centennial of the detective story, suggests that a detective story or novel must have a central figure, professional or amateur, who is engaged primarily in the detection of crime. Mr. Haycraft goes on to point out that only a democratic society, possessed of a police force, and dedicated to the equal administration of justice, could produce a milieu which would insist on the solution of crime by logical methods of proof and evidence. In fact, the first modern societies to fit those specifications were France, England, and America of the nineteenth century, inspired, no doubt, by the Enlightenment of the previous century.

In simpler terms, the role of the detective is to find out whodunit, whatever crime the "it" may be. As with every literary form, certain conventions have grown up. The reader must be given all the clues necessary to solve the crime himself, but they must be cunningly presented so that he sees them without realising their significance. However, if the puzzle were the entire interest of the story, a finished detective novel would hold no more excitement than a finished crossword puzzle in yesterday's newspaper and, in point of fact, a second-rate detective story does get thrown out with yesterday's newspaper. But those who condemn the detective story as artificial because it contains a puzzle to be solved miss the vital key which explains the continuing popularity of the genre.

That key is the well-made plot. The term "well made" usually refers to a play, and is defined by Beckson and Ganz in *A Reader's Guide to Literary Terms* thus:

> The plot of a well-made play regularly revolves about a secret known only to some of the characters; revealed at the climax, it leads to the downfall of the villain and the triumph of the hero. The action, which centers on a conflict—especially a duel of wits—between the hero and his opponent, builds with increasing intensity through a series of reversals which culminate in the climactic revelation scene. Misunderstandings, compromising letters, precisely timed entrances and exits, and other such devices contribute to the suspense. The *dénouement* is always carefully prepared, and, within the framework of the manipulated action, believable.

That quotation could serve very well as the definition of the detective story. In point of fact, the detective author must have every detail plotted in his mind before he sets a word down on paper. He must have the crime worked out in both directions—from the inception to the execution, as carried out by the criminal, and from the discovery back to what must have been the planning stages, as worked out by the detective. Only if he has done this necessary spadework will the author be able to scatter real clues and worthless clues, making both seem equally important, at the same time that he is making sure his characters are all in the right place at the right time. Every detail must be explained by or in the last chapter, and every one of the characters accounted for in such a way that the bad are punished and the good rewarded—no small feat when you stop to consider that all through the book we have been unsure which were which. Furthermore, the reader's interest must be captured and held, lest he get bored and skip ahead (ruinous to any well-made plot!). In other words, every good detective story or novel must have a plot that is at least as complicated as *Oedipus Rex* and *The Importance of Being Earnest*. It is this well-made plot to which readers refer when they say that they like a detective novel "because it tells a story," unlike many contemporary "straight" novels. They enjoy, in fact, that aspect of drama contained in a classical plot: the inception of action, the rising to a climax, and the final dramatic resolution. When they finish the book, they have the feeling of having been somewhere, of having taken a trip that didn't end back where they started. It is perhaps unwise to draw ill-formed psychological conclusions as to why detective stories are popular, but the fact that they were so much in demand in air-raid shelters in London during the blitz suggests, perhaps, that people in times of crisis like to be able to live briefly in a well-ordered world, one which shows clearly the work of a creator who is above all else logical.

Perfectly obviously there are twentieth-century "straight" novels with well-made plots—William Humphrey's brilliantly worked-out *Home from the*

Hill comes instantly to mind. But it is interesting that Humphrey's novel, like the detective story, finds its inspiration in classic Greek tragedy: a central figure feels that he is more powerful and intelligent than other human beings. He breaks the moral code, and his cockiness, his *hubris,* does him in at the end.

By no means are all detective novels the artistic equal of Greek tragedy. Many never rise above the level of rather mediocre puzzles. For one thing, some authors discover that one formula or story pattern works, and they then proceed to run it into the ground. The late Willard Huntington Wright (S. S. Van Dine) is a case in point. The first Van Dine book one reads is always enjoyable, except for the dated slang, but even the most dim-witted reader soon discovers thereafter that if you pair the characters off into the obvious amorous matches, the odd man out is your murderer.

Furthermore, some detective writers forget that a well-made plot consists essentially of a battle of wits, and they introduce a *deus ex machina* in the form of scientific gadgetry. Here the late Ian Fleming is a case in point. When the author relies on such devices, his stories will date very rapidly. For instance, one of the least successful Sherlock Holmes stories is the one in which Holmes convinces the criminal that the famous detective is still present by playing a phonograph record of a violin solo. And it is rather hard in the 1960's to get excited about a 1920ish story in which people evade their pursuers by attaining the utterly fantastic speed of 90 miles an hour. One fears that Fleming's James Bond will be rather dated in an age when everyone has his own portable flying suit.

Yet when an author eschews gadgetry, and concentrates on the never-changing mental and thought processes of his characters, his books are much less likely to fall by the wayside. Agatha Christie's first detective novel, *The Mysterious Affair at Styles,* was written in 1915 and published in 1920—seven years before the last Sherlock Holmes short story collection appeared in book form. Mrs. Christie has produced a mystery novel or short story collection at the rate of at least one a year ever since 1920, and one might well imagine that the early books would be somewhat dated by this point. Surprisingly enough, they are not, and practically all Mrs. Christie's books are kept perpetually in print in either paperback or omnibus editions. A career which exceeds forty-five years in length is remarkable in any field, but is especially noteworthy in the field of so-called "popular" literature, for it would seem that people's tastes would change radically in that span of time.

Mrs. Christie has certain rules, ploys, and formulas. To a certain extent, some of the rules are inherent in the detective story as a form, as we have suggested. Other patterns or gambits seem to grow up as the form matures. This is by no means a phenomenon unique to the detective story—the sonnet is a prime example of a literary form or pattern which has served for centuries as both a challenge and an inspiration to writers. Yet the detective story or novel

must at once display and conceal its form, lest the
reader arrive at the solution to the problem at hand
sooner than he is meant to do. But enough of theory,
let us get down to cases.

CHAPTER TWO

The Career of
Agatha Christie Mallowan

AGATHA CHRISTIE finds it hard to be specific about just how she creates the plots which consistently baffle her readers. To a certain extent, it is difficult for any naturally talented person to explain how he comes by his talent. He soon learns the folly of saying "I don't know—it's just *easy*." For it is easy for a musician with perfect pitch to recognise a 440 A every time that he hears one, but very difficult for him to explain just why or how he can recognise and identify the sound so easily. Well-coordinated athletes are hard put to it to explain why they are good at tennis or golf, and as yet psychology has not been able to take the creative process in the arts and separate it into all of its component parts. It may, in fact, be that creativity is a gift, or a talent, as that latter word is used symbolically in the New Testament.

Not unnaturally, those who have been interested in

the creative talent which Agatha Christie displays have sought some clue from her childhood. But here, Mrs. Christie maintains, they have been somewhat misled in that they have compared her background with that of a child brought up in the mid-twentieth century. By mid-twentieth-century standards, she had an unusually solitary childhood. She was the second daughter of an Anglo-American marriage, and her father, the American, died when she was little. Nigel Dennis in his *Life Magazine* article about Agatha Christie (1956), implies that Mrs. Miller (Agatha's mother) tutored Agatha at home. In this day and age of super-organised activity for children, Mrs. Miller's actions would seem to many to be the height of cruelty, but it is well worth remembering that the American child who is whisked from school to ballet class to little league baseball to clarinet lessons never has a chance to learn to do anything really well. In an age when we have confused meditation with idleness, the idea of leaving a child alone with a book, or just alone to think, seems almost sacrilegious.

However, Mrs. Christie suggests that even in the period from 1890 to 1905 children were not quite so idle as we might conclude today from the fact that they were not sent out to school. She says, "At that time, girls very rarely went to school—it would have been thought a very odd thing to do! My elder sister, who was sent to 'the Miss Lawences at Brighton'—a pioneer school (afterwards Roedean)—created great surprise that Mr. and Mrs. Miller should have done such an extraordinary thing! All my friends had first a nurse or nursery maid, a nursery governess—later a governess or foreign nursery governess or sewing maid, more to look after or companion a child than to teach. As education, one had 'classes.' You went to Dancing Class—Swedish Exercises—Art School—Piano Lessons—Singing Class—Cookery Classes, etc. All I escaped was a resident governess—and certainly my mother was much better fun."

Yet the young Agatha Miller did have the time to investigate books and develop a liking for romance, fairy stories, Dickens, and Sherlock Holmes. Two events seem to stand out in her mind as high-water marks or influential moments—the first when she was ill in bed one time and her mother encouraged her to write a short story, which she did and found she enjoyed. The second event occurred about 1915, when her elder sister made a remark which surely must rank along with the challenge given Mary Shelley at dinner one night. In Mary Shelley's case, someone said that horror stories were difficult to do, and Mrs. Shelley (so the legend goes) rose to the occasion and said that she'd do one on a bet. Dr. Frankenstein and his nameless monster were the result of the challenge, and few people would dare to suggest that Mrs. Shelley did not win the bet hands down. Agatha Christie's sister said simply, "I bet you can't write a good detective story." It was a fortunate and stimulating challenge. For one thing, Agatha Christie had been writing up to that time "stories of unrelieved gloom, in which most of the characters died," according to her own admission. Secondly, having taken First Aid and Home Nursing Certificates, she joined a Voluntary Aid Detachment and worked in the Red Cross Hospital on the outbreak of the 1914 War, first as a nurse and then as a dispenser. (Her experiences along this line are suggested in *The Mysterious Affair at Styles*.) She gained from this work, in addition to a feeling of holy terror for the sisters in authority, a very good working knowledge of poisons, as the following poem, entitled "In a Dispensary," suggests. The poem comes from a privately printed collection entitled *Road of Dreams*, published in the early 1920's by Geoffrey Bles of London. Unfortunately, no American edition has ever existed.

IN A DISPENSARY

Oh! who shall say where Romance is, if
     Romance is not here?
For here are Colour, Death and Sleep . . .
     and Magic everywhere!

Glistening salts, and shimmering scales, and
     crystals of purest white,
High on the shelves in their spotless rows,
     enclosed in their bottles bright,
Salts of iron of palest green, or deepening
     down to brown,
And many a tincture, many a wine, from far-
     off lands unknown . . .

Light as a promise, and bitter as sin—that
     feathery foam, Quinine
And sedate beside it, in silver and black, the
     sea-born Iodine;

Soon shall it merge to orange and brown in a
    rich and widening hue
Which perchance, in far-off Tyrian days, the
    old Phoenicians knew.

Here heavy syrups, thick and sweet, pre-
    pared with skill and toil,
And there, distilled in precious drops, stands
    many a spicèd oil:
Lavender, Nutmeg and Sandalwood; Cin-
    namon, Clove and Pine,
While above, in palest primrose hue, the
    Flowers of Sulphur shine.

And high on the wall, beneath lock and
    key, the powers of the Quick and
    Dead!
Little low bottles of blue and green, *each
    with a legend red.*
In the depths beneath their slender necks,
    there is Romance, and to spare!
*Oh! who shall say where Romance is, if
    Romance is not here?*

From the Borgia's time to the present
    day, their power has been proved and
    tried!
Monkshood blue, called Aconite, and the
    deadly cyanide!
Here is sleep and solace and soothing of pain
    —courage and vigour new!
Here is menace and murder and sudden
    death!—in these phials of green and
    blue!

Here are copper salts that shame the
    heavens, and sparkle deep and blue,

And never a Mediterranean Sea shall match
    their Sapphire hue!
And oh! the many dazzling dyes—the
    golden-hued Flavine,
And the fine bronze dust that shall turn at
    will to a glory of Brilliant Green!

A philtre of Love—a philtre of Death—were
    they only a Sorcerer's lore?
To catch the pence, and trap the fool? Or
    were they something more?
Beware of the Powers that never die, though
    Men may go their way,
The Power of the Drug, for good or ill, shall
    it ever pass away?

Oh! who shall say where Romance is, if
    Romance is not here?
For here are Colour, Death and Sleep . . .
    and Magic everywhere!

While Agatha Chirstie was working at the Red
Cross Hospital in Torquay, she had a chance to ob-
serve more than poisons. England was at the time engaged in the resettlement of Belgian refugees, and
a group of these people were billeted near Torquay.
Agatha Christie was not the only writer aspiring
to carry on the torch lighted by Conan Doyle. In
this country, for example, Robert Barr looked around
for an eccentric detective to lend character to his
stories, and he seized upon the idea of a retired
French detective of enormous ego, whom he christened Eugène Valmont, and who appeared in a short
story collection by Mr. Barr entitled (modestly) *The*

Triumphs of Eugène Valmont. Agatha Christie, working, as it turns out, quite independently, ten years later, conceived of the idea of a retired foreign detective of superhuman ego who would lend an exotic air to London. She chose the nearest thing at hand—one of the Belgian refugees, and how Hercule Poirot, lately retired from the Brussels police force, came to England is detailed in *Styles*. Mrs. Christie readily acknowledges her debt to Conan Doyle, but says that she knew of Barr's work and was rather unimpressed by it. She preferred, she says, "the Sherlock Holmes form of construction, i.e., detective with idiosyncrasies and also with respectable, nice, but idiotic friend." The "idiotic friend" referred to is of course Capt. Arthur Hastings, whom Howard Haycraft has called "easily the stupidest of the modern Watsons." Mrs. Christie evidently tired of him, for she banished him to the Argentine in the late 1930's.

Armed, then, with her love of Sherlock Holmes and of storytelling, her working knowledge of poisons, and her casual acquaintance with the nearby Belgian refugees ("I doubt if I ever actually met any of them!" Mrs. Christie confides), Agatha Christie set out to meet her sister's challenge. *The Mysterious Affair at Styles* was promptly rejected by the first six publishers that saw it, but finally John Lane of the Bodley Head in London decided to take a gamble and publish it. His gamble paid off handsomely, and the writer Sutherland Scott has dubbed the book "one of the finest firsts ever written."

Although she says that she did not seriously con-

sider making a living out of writing until she had
sold five or six books, Agatha Christie did derive a
good deal of pleasure and a not inconsiderable re-
muneration during the early 1920's from her writing, as her books came out at about the rate of one
a year. She and her husband christened their house
at Sunningdale, Berkshire, "Styles" after the success
of the first novel, and Agatha Christie expressed much
delight at owning her first car—a bottle-nosed Morris.
She had become engaged some years previously, in
1912, to Archibald Christie, whom she married in
1914. She had joined the Voluntary Aid Detachment
when he was sent on active duty in France as a
Colonel in the Royal Flying Corps, and they had been
reunited at the close of the war. All seemed to be
going smoothly in 1926 when *The Murder of Roger
Ackroyd* appeared. At this point, the detective story
was still an even newer and more untried form than
it is today, and Mrs. Christie simply thought up the
idea of having one of the central characters hitherto
considered above suspicion turn out to be the murderer. The detective world was rent in twain, with
people crying "Foul!" and others, such as the mystery
novelist Dorothy Sayers, crying "Fair! and Fooled
you!"

Hard on the heels of this, Agatha Christie's mother
died, and Agatha Christie sensed the impending
breakup of her own marriage. These two pressures,
together with the strain of constant work, became too
much for her inventive mind to absorb all at once,
and it revolted in one of the curious ways that minds

have to relieve anxiety. Agatha Christie suffered an attack of amnesia, and simply walked out of her life one afternoon in 1926, abandoning her car in a field.

The amnesia has since been verified beyond any shadow of a doubt as genuine, but at the time there were doubts indeed among the general public. An anonymous tip led police to a hotel in Harrogate, Yorkshire, where a young lady was staying under an assumed name. The young lady, who was reported as being eager to play piano in trios with the orchestra there, turned out to be Agatha Christie, registered under the name of the woman who later became Colonel Christie's second wife.

What stung Mrs. Christie most about the whole unfortunate incident was that the press had accused her of disappearing as a publicity stunt to advertise her books, although why in the name of heaven she would have registered under the name she did if it were a publicity stunt never seemed to occur to people at the time.

It is a sad fact of life that the British press has been known upon occasion to be very cruel to famous people—American actresses constantly object to having the less happy aspects of their past pointed out to them in print as soon as they arrive in London.

To a certain extent, Mrs. Christie's desire for privacy has only fanned the flames of curiosity since 1926. For many years she sought to avoid any publicity whatsoever, and would not even let her publishers print her portrait with her books. She has said on numerous occasions that she feels authors (unlike actresses) ought to remain "background, shadowy figures," and, considering her unfortunate experience with publicity in 1926, one can certainly sympathise with her. Furthermore, some journalists (including those on a prominent Paris weekly) have resorted from time to time to telephoto lenses to take pictures of Mrs. Christie as she sits eating in a restaurant, or as she comes out of one of her houses. Anyone who has ever had candid photos snapped of him unawares knows that most often the results are considerably less than flattering, and Mrs. Christie feels most decidedly that the pictures in question of her are that.

However, with the passing of time, Mrs. Christie has mellowed her views to the extent that she will grant interviews to responsible journalists who have the good taste to present their credentials to her agents and arrange for a mutually convenient interview—Nigel Dennis, Francis Wyndham, and the present author are three cases in point. For Mrs. Christie is very grateful for the affection and admiration in which she is held by her readers, and is not aloof but shy, as she suggests in her 1946 autobiographical *Come, Tell Me How You Live.*

Mrs. Christie divorced Col. Archibald Christie in 1928; he died in 1962. By this marriage she had a daughter, Rosalind, who, she says, "is my severest critic—and guesses the outcome of all my plots." On a holiday in Mesopotamia in 1930, she met Max Mallowan, an archaeologist on the expedition led by Sir Leonard Woolley to reconstruct the ancient Sumerian city of Ur. She and Professor Mallowan were married in September 1930, and have lived very happily ever since. *She accompany us~~always~~ on his~~city~~ in the middle east*

Mrs. Christie (for she has kept this as her professional name) has never been one for letting good experience or knowledge go to waste. For many years she accompanied Professor Mallowan on his excursions to the Middle East, and used the settings as background for several of what she calls her "foreign travel books"—*Death on the Nile, Murder in Mesopotamia,* and *Appointment with Death* are but three examples. Nor has she confined herself to the goings-on in the Middle East: she considers the getting there to be worthy of note as well, and satisfies the romantic wanderlust of her readers by chronicling train journies across Europe and the Middle East—*The Mystery of the Blue Train* and *Murder on the Orient Express* come immediately to mind, although the reader who wishes to read all the novels in a certain category can make up his own complete list from the material given in Appendix B.

During the Second World War, Mrs. Christie again worked in a dispensary, this time in London in University College Hospital. Her husband, Professor Mallowan, had joined the Royal Air Force, but was "seconded," or loaned out, by that organisation to the British Military government in North Africa to act as Advisor on Arab Affairs in Tripolitania. As Mrs. Christie said in her interview in the London *Sunday Times* with Francis Wyndham, there was little to do evenings during the war except write, and the war years showed the production of two of her most ingenious books, *The Labours of Hercules*, in which M. Poirot takes twelve cases to provide mental counterparts for his namesake's physical tasks, and *Death Comes as the End*, a *tour de force* set in Egypt in 2000 B.C., which required, as Mrs. Christie has said, "endless research on everyday details." In addition, these years produced the two posthumous novels, one a Poirot and the other a Miss Marple which will appear as the last books in their respective series as a sad farewell—we hope not for a good many years.

The Mallowans own at present two houses—Greenway House in Devonshire (pictured in the illustrations in this book); Winterbrook House, a smaller residence near Oxford; and they have a small flat in Chelsea for the occasions when they come up to London. Mrs. Mallowan in person is a large woman who gives the impression of being quite tall. She wears her grey hair pulled into an enormous French knot at the back of her head, and her blue eyes sparkle from behind her glasses. She still has a rather high soprano voice (she took singing lessons in Paris during her teens) and is quite shrewd and alert. The sense of humour which enlivens her books is apparent from her conversation, and she keeps up her interests in music and cooking. Her husband's book *Nimrud and Its Remains,* the culmination of thirty-five years' research in the Middle East, is dedicated to her and together with Mrs. Mallowan's own *Come,*

Tell Me How You Live, provides a delightful (and colourful) insight into a shared career.

Two mistakes which have been perpetuated ought to be rectified. There have been, in fact, factual inaccuracies in articles about Mrs. Christie for years, and they are copied and recopied to the extent that it would almost be easier to change the facts to fit the fictions, and the present author is as guilty as anyone. It would be a great help to scholarship if all editors would checks their facts with Hughes Massie, Mrs. Christie's agents, before assuming anything to be true, and certainly before copying anything out of a previously published article. For instance, if we must know the date of Mrs. Christie's birth for library cards, it is 1890, and not 1891, in spite of all the library cards to the contrary; and the wrong date in fact appeared in my own article "Perdurable Agatha" in *The New York Times Book Review* in November 1965. Furthermore, the remark attributed to Mrs. Christie that "the older you get, the more interesting you become to an archaeologist" was the creation of some pundit whose neck Mrs. Christie would be glad to wring if he would care to identify himself— she neither made the remark nor does she consider it particularly complimentary or amusing.

But in spite of all the inaccuracies and invasions of privacy, Mrs. Christie looks back upon the first half century of her career with fondness and affection for her readers, although she admits to being a little awed at the idea that she must produce a Christie for

Christmas each year lest the earth veer off its course. "A sausage machine, a perfect sausage machine," she calls herself.

But then, as she re-reads some of her favourite mystery authors and spots a trick she likes, she closes the book with a twinkle in her eye and says, "You know, it would be rather fun if I could do that. . . ."

CHAPTER THREE

Mystery Writers as
Social Historians

ENTHUSIASTS OF THE detective story and novel may
take comfort from the prediction of the late Somer-
set Maugham that the day will come when detective
novels will be studied in colleges, and aspirants for
doctor's degrees "shuttle oceans and haunt the world's
great libraries to conduct personal expeditions into
the lives and sources of the masters of the art." Mr.
Maugham even went so far on one occasion as to suggest that the detective story will be regarded as the
twentieth century's greatest contribution to literature.

This, as we suggested in the first chapter, may remain for the twenty-first century to decide, for the
novel as a popular form did not suffer from too much
scholarly attention in the nineteenth century, when
it was still as new as the detective story is today. Yet
when one goes back to the early Christies, one must
agree with Maureen Smith, who said in her article
"The Deadly Ladies" (*New York Herald Tribune,*

27 March 1966) that Ruth Fenisong, the American mystery novelist, may have hit upon the value of the mystery novel to future generations. Miss Fenisong believes that mysteries give later generations a vivid and accurate day-to-day picture of life in a society.

At first blush this would seem to be an absurd statement. After all, most members of any society have little to do with robbery, and still less with murder. Yet, in order to make murder believable, mystery authors go to no little pains to make their backgrounds (and their caricatures) seem real, and attention to daily detail is an important means to this end. Miss Fenisong cites Mary Roberts Rinehart as a vivid chronicler of American upper-class life between the two world wars, when people took it as a matter of course that their summer cottages would have servants, and a quick lunch consisted of a three-course affair served at the dining room table by at least one servant. And she lauds Agatha Christie for her presentation of life in an English village during the same period, which is commendable but hardly a comprehensive account of Mrs. Christie's skill in settings. It is, perhaps, the changes which Mrs. Christie chronicles in English life which will be the most useful to future historians. For instance, consider *The Secret Adversary,* Mrs. Christie's second book (1920), which introduced her bold young heroes —Tommy and Tuppence Beresford. Tommy and his girl (Tuppence Cowley) come into unexpected funds at the beginning of Chapter III. Tuppence is hungry, and so the adventuresome duo sallies forth to the *Piccadilly,* where they lunch on "hors d'oeuvres, lobster à l'américaine, chicken Newburg, and pêche Melba."

Surprisingly, they survived the luncheon, but Tommy caught a glimpse of a sinister figure met before: Whittington! Undaunted, Tommy trailed Whittington and his companion, and "they crossed the road, Tommy, unperceived, faithfully at their heels, and entered the big Lyons'. Tommy took a seat at the table next to them. . . . Having already lunched heartily, Tommy contented himself with ordering a Welsh rarebit and a cup of coffee."

That society did not fade with the setting of the sun on the British Empire. It died of indigestion!

But Tommy and Tuppence survived to produce the twins who thought their parents hopelessly old-fashioned in *N or M?* (1941), and Mrs. Christie has hinted that perhaps they may reappear as grandparents soon. One hopes they will, for it will undoubtedly mark the first time that people have appeared in detective fiction at least in three different generations—each generation's novel separated by the proper length of time for the intervening generations to grow up. Agatha Christie knows perfectly well what the younger generation is thinking today—her grandson Mathew Prichard is about the age of Tommy and Tuppence's grandchildren, and she has put that knowledge to good use in *At Bertram's Hotel* (1965), which casually mentions the fashion note that a young lady appears dressed in a shift. The observation (and the young lady's comments) appear obvious enough in the mid-1960's, but I wonder how many of Mrs. Christie's readers under thirty know what a lace fichu is? (Miss Marple appeared in them in her early books in the 1930's, and according to ladies old enough to remember Miss Marple's original generation, she might well have done this.) It is true that the world will not rise or fall on the matter of a lace fichu (or a shift), but if future historians wish to find out how breakfast was served in English country houses after World War I, they will get more information and background about the system in operation from *The Secret of Chimneys* and *The Seven Dials Mystery* than any cookery book or historical text can provide. For this reason, it is wise not to read Agatha Christie late at night if one is dieting. After a particularly mouth-watering breakfast or luncheon scene, one is apt to think, "You know, it would be rather fun if I could do that. . . ."

And even if one has the will power to stave off kidneys, eggs and bacon, sausage and omelettes, one is apt to end up having at least a sandwich.

Aside from cookery and fashion, the oddest notes crop up in Christie works. For instance, one thinks (at least in the United States) of electricity as being relatively common in urban and suburban areas by the time of World War I. Yet Styles evidently cooked with gas and lighted with lanterns as late as the middle of the war, and Styles was drawn to represent an English way of life that thought cutting down for the war consisted of taking coffee black and reducing the gardening staff from five men to three!

When some seventh-grade students in Newton, Massachusetts, were given the task of writing their version of the last chapter of *Roger Ackroyd* in 1966, forty years after the book's conception, they replaced the eight pages extracted from their books with accounts in which Dr. Sheppard drives all over the place in his car. And one student, eager to express disdain, had Dr. Sheppard exclaim, "So this is all there is to it? I could have stayed at home and watched *Peyton Place* on TV!"

Evidently the world changes rapidly. Of course, it will be possible for future historians to consult Sears, Roebuck catalogues to determine the price of nylon stockings in 1940, the London *Times* to determine how Englishmen thought of the Chinese as a race in 1926, and statistical tables to determine how many people of the young married set overextended themselves to buy appliances on Hire-Purchase (time payment) plans in English villages in the 1960's. But what newspapers, catalogues, and tables will never tell us is how these various details fitted into the life of the average well-educated member of the middle class in England (or America) at those times. It remains for the novelist to fill in this blank section of the canvas, and as the detective novelist must be concerned with painting a vivid and realistic everyday background to serve as camouflage for his plot and clues, one can see that Ruth Fenisong may perhaps have a point in her assertion that the detective novel will be of great use to social historians.

CHAPTER FOUR

Devices of the Profession

ALTHOUGH Agatha Christie's mysteries remain remarkably consistent in their appeal to readers, it is quite possible to notice some changes, or advances, in the manner and style of mystery writing from 1920 to the present day. The field is still a young and fertile one, and the books which both the Crime Club of England and the Mystery Writers of America have put out as anthologies of how-to-write-mysteries are quite specific in stating that for every rule and maxim many exceptions can be found in the works of first-rate authors. The serious student of the mystery story and novel as a literary form will be undoubtedly quite interested in the very readable texts cited in the bibliography of this book, and the general mystery fan may well increase his enjoyment by stopping to consider how it's all done, and what the masters have to say upon the subject. It is interesting to note that the authors of the few scholarly essays on the mystery seem to have taken notice of Alexander Pope's remark from the *Essay on Criticism:* "Men must be taught as if you taught them not/ And things unknown proposed as things forgot."

By this they do not mean by any means to suggest that the writing of a mystery story is easy. It is not; in fact, any serious intellectual endeavour demands time, concentration, discipline, and training, and anyone who thinks that good mystery novels can just be tossed off might try tossing one off for fun some weekend. Yet it is commendable that writers of stature and success will take the time to try to interest and instruct the tyro in terms that he can understand, for by no means is all knowledge contained within the cloisters of the university, and scholarship does not have to be dull. Learning can be fun, and at any age. It is true that some popularisers of knowledge are out-and-out charlatans and are rightly shunned by serious scholars, but on the other hand, we must remember that if the serious scholars took more pains to interest the general knowledgeable public in their field, the scholars would command more attention, and their fields more respect. In fact, their salaries might even go up!

So the general mystery fan should not shun the technical books on the subject that interests him for his leisure reading. He will learn much, and appreciate what he enjoys even more.

For instance, he will find out that diagrams, maps, and Watsons have been out of vogue since the 1930's. Why? It is often suggested that all three items have been worn out and overused, but this is a dangerous explanation, even in a field where formulas, plot devices, and conventions are building blocks (and, more than occasionally, stumbling blocks). The answer perhaps lies in the fact that as the mystery story as a form becomes more mature and sophisticated, so do its readers. They can keep in their heads as many details as the detective can, and as the author is honour-bound to note every detail that is of importance when describing a scene, the reader may justly assume that the author's eyes are as good as his own would be—in fact, better. The Watson, or amanuensis, presents a very real problem of identification. Generally, the scribe and detective's friend is stupider than the detective, and after he has been proven deficient in little grey cells several times, the reader longs to get this stupid friend out of the way and take his place, in order to solve the mystery better and faster. If, on the other hand, the Watson is presented as being as smart as the detective, or as being a really potential suspect, the reader is likely to feel cheated at the end, and the particular Watson will have outlived his usefulness as the final curtain falls on the first book in which he appears. This latter situation, in fact, was the basis for the one really great controversy which has broken out over Agatha Christie's books, and although that Watson-for-one-occasion can never reappear, Mrs. Christie would be justified in pulling the same stunt once again; in fact, as she originated the twist, she is perhaps the one author who could duplicate it without incurring a charge of plagiarism.

It is very difficult to know where to draw the line

between borrowed inspiration and plagiarism in the field of the detective story. Every detective author acknowledges his or her debt to Edgar Allan Poe and Arthur Conan Doyle, and Agatha Christie constantly has her earlier characters accuse each other of having read too much G. K. Chesterton for their own good.

Imitation is always the sincerest form of flattery, and detective stories do supply inspiration for more detective stories. For instance, we spoke earlier of two kinds of clues: important clues and worthless ones. The worthless clues, or red herrings, seem to be important, but really are laid solely to mislead and confuse the reader (and the detective). But an ingenious author would soon get the idea of writing a story using the same basic characters or plot, and making one small but important change: this time, the previously worthless clues will turn out to be the important ones, and the hitherto important clues will be made into red herrings.

And no detective author would mind supplying another with this kind of inspiration, provided the imitator added a new fillip of plot, or an interesting change of scene—many authors, including Agatha Christie, borrow even from themselves in this way, and make the later books acknowledge the characters and detectives in the earlier ones. In point of fact, this is the means by which Mrs. Christie has created many of her "series."

We have thus far been dealing pretty much with abstract theory in this chapter. It is indeed possible to cite specific examples to make the theories clear, but such citations would get us into perhaps the greatest problem in discussing the detective story critically. In Chapter I we discussed the two reasons why many scholars feel the detective novel is not worthy of consideration: first, that it is popular and therefore inferior, and secondly, that it relies on artificial plots and caricatures. Those hardy souls who have attempted scholarly discussions of the form have at once found that they are dealing with a literary genre having one unique convention. In the case of the well-made play or the straight novel, it is "permissible" to give away the ending, for most well-made plays and straight novels do not rely heavily on the factor of suspense. Yet the detective novel does, and many inferior detective novels, as we said, are good only for one reading—when the murderer is unmasked, out they go with the trash.

However, to see exactly how a detective plot is put together, and how the theories of borrowing as opposed to plagiarism work out in actual practice, we must dissect a detective novel and consider it in both the directions in which it runs—from the discovery of the crime to the unmasking of the murderer (forwards), and from the murderer's foul planning to his final downfall (backwards). It is the fact of the detective novel being written, as we said, in both directions at once that makes the critic's and student's task so vexing.

However, the difficulty is far from insuperable. Let us choose one vintage Christie, *The A.B.C. Murders,* and devote a chapter to the consideration of it: the idea that insipred it, the imagination that executed it, and the imitators that have copied it. Those of you who have never read this particular Poirot, or who want to brush up on it before discussing it, skip Chapter VII of this book for the time being, for you will find the dénouement mentioned nowhere else within these pages. Having refreshed your memory with a re-reading of the assigned text, you can peruse the chapter in question with all of the facts fresh in mind. Or, if you have read or re-read *A.B.C.* recently and want to skip ahead to the chapter now, you will find it pretty much a self-contained unit.

But as we are concerned with tricks and devices at the moment, let us stick to these. Agatha Christie said in her interview with Francis Wyndham that she "probably could write the same book again and again, and nobody would notice." That, of course, is not strictly true. But it is very true that devices used once can be used again. For instance, *Towards Zero, The Mirror Crack'd,* and *A Caribbean Mystery* all feature strongly the idea of intense surprise when a person looks straight ahead of him over another person's shoulder and is shocked or stunned by what he sees. The question we are supposed to figure out is, "What did he or she see which made him so upset?" In all three cases, the scene has been described vividly enough so that we have been presented with everything that was within the person's line of vision. The puzzler is: Which of the persons or objects is the important one, and why? However, in two of the three books cited, the person doing the looking is a future victim; in one, it is the murderer. And in all three cases, we are given elsewhere in the book the clue that should supply the right answer as to both the who and the why of the question. Naturally, that clue is not trumpeted from the housetops: it is tossed out in casual conversation. Yet as the detective must pick the needle out of the haystack, so must we.

Agatha Christie has been accused of overusing the "least-likely-person motif." But she enjoys playing with her readers, and delights in using the most-likely-person motif as well, sometimes having our clever murderer arrange a whole set of false evidence to be discovered against himself, having taken care to provide an alibi to be released at the most dramatic moment to clear himself, on the shrewd assumption that having been cleared once, he will forever remain above suspicion thereafter. It would be a little unfair to future readers of Christie to be specific about the books in which this device appears; let us say rather that of the four titles mentioned thus far in this chapter, one is a prime example of the device, as is one of the earliest Miss Marple books.

It is dangerous for the reader to attempt the sort of equation-solving in Agatha Christie's books that is so often successful in the novels of S. S. Van Dine. It is true that if an American actress figures prominently in a Christie book, the reader does well to scrutinise her movements and motives very well, for on two different occasions the actress has turned out to be a completely selfish and unprincipled murderess, which is a pretty high batting average, considering that American actresses, particularly film actresses, have not appeared in very many more than two Christies. Doctors, lawyers, justices, n'er-do-well sons and relatives, mothers, and children have all ended up in the dock, as have Poirot's companions in the solution of murder. Victims have been known to be guilty of murder—*Ten Little Niggers (And Then There Were None)* is the best-known example of victim-murderer. In fact, and this may be going out on a limb which Mrs. Christie will delightedly saw off, the only "type" so far above reproach is a clergyman of the Church of England. Beyond that, as Dorothy Sayers said after the publication of *The Murder of Roger Ackroyd,* "it is the reader's business to suspect *everybody.*"

We have mentioned Mrs. Christie's repetition of characters from one book to another, and the warm feeling of friendship which this creates in her readers. This practice began early in the 1920's, when *The Secret of Chimneys* introduced Lord Caterham, his butler named Tredwell (shades of Sheridan's appropriately named characters!), and the large country estate Chimneys, which seemed to attract international intrigue and murder the way a-magnet attracts metal. The house and its inhabitants return shortly thereafter in *The Seven Dials Mystery,* when Lord Caterham decided not to rent out his estate to any more self-made millionaires. Supt. Battle appears in *Seven Dials,* re-appears prominently several times; for instance in *Towards Zero,* and even after the good Superintendent retires he is not gone and forgotten—his son takes up detection in *The Clocks* twenty years later (1963) under the assumed name of Colin Lamb, so as not to be accused of pulling rank with his father's reputation. Lamb, incidentally, is not identified as Battle's son in *The Clocks;* Mrs. Christie unmasked him (with a twinkle in her eye) in response to a question from this author.

One wishes that the major detectives themselves could meet, for a conversation between Miss Marple and Hercule Poirot would be fascinating—they are both shrewd enough to respect each other. *The Regatta Mystery and Other Stories* (American only, 1939) has been advertised as "featuring Hercule Poirot, Miss Marple, and Parker Pyne," which is somewhat misleading—the detectives, although present, do not in fact meet within the covers of the book, and the film version of *The A.B.C. Murders* had no business bringing Miss Marple into the act in even a cameo role, although it was of course delightful to see Margaret Rutherford once again.

Some little attention has been given to the fact that Mrs. Christie is quite skilful in presenting Chesterton-type situations in which the reader sees only what he is meant to see. For instance, in the relatively early short story and later novel chapter, "The Importance of a Leg of Mutton" from *The Big Four,* the witnesses did not see anyone enter the cottage in question. Yet a particularly brutal murder was committed, and the murderer must have left with blood on his clothes. No one, they reiterated, had come to the house that morning except the butcher.

And as the butcher came to the house with regularity, he was not noticed or counted as "anybody." Needless to say, the gentleman in butcher's uniform who left with blood on his apron that morning was not the real butcher, who had been waylaid, but actually one of The Big Four—the executioner.

Another famous Christie example appears not to have been created by Agatha Christie but rather by Nigel Dennis in his 1956 *Life* article—at least, no one has been able to find the "elusive short-sighted butler" in any of Mrs. Christie's works. The incident (typical of many, but apparently quite original) concerns a conversation between Poirot and a butler:

> Has the date been taken off a certain calendar since the murder? Poirot asks the butler. The butler crosses the room, peers at the calendar, and gives his answer. The reader tucks this suggestion of *dates* carefully away for future reference—and misses the point to perfection. The butler has demonstrated that he is too short-sighted to see across the room, a point of crucial importance to the plot.

There is an example of a typical Christie clue which works two ways. The obvious explanation is the wrong one, the red herring; and the subtle explanation, right in front of the reader's eyes, so to speak, is the true one. No one can say that he has been cheated. In yet another story Poirot buys a quantity of silk stockings, and arranges them in disarray on a table. He asks a young lady to choose the most expensive pair, which she is glad to do when Poirot leaves her alone for a few moments to complete the task. After she leaves, it seems that she has shown the cards in her hand rather too clearly: there are two fewer pairs of stockings on the table than there were when she came in. Poirot has discovered what he wanted: she is a petty thief.

In the game of Patience which detective readers play, they must be able to remember who has spoken and written to whom and how and why. For instance, in Mrs. Christie's fiftieth book, *A Murder Is Announced,* much should be made of the fact that "enquire" is sometimes spelt "inquire." A small point, and one doubtless meant to make readers think that the printers have been at it again with their peculiar version of mid-Atlantic spelling that leaves the "u" in glamour and takes it out of colour, for, after all, "practise" and "practice" mean two quite different things in England.

Diagrams, as mentioned previously, have been out of vogue since the 1930's. Accordingly, when Mrs. Christie uses one in 1963 in *The Clocks,* the reader had better not think that she is going senile. He had better consider the thing from all angles.

If, however, one had to think of two devices which Mrs. Christie has used over and over again most ingeniously, they surely would be the nursery rhyme as an organising theme, and spiritualism as a cover for a perfectly straightforward crime.

Mrs. Christie has evidently found in nursery rhymes an inspiration which permits her to develop plots with built-in suspense: the reader knows that the murderer is following the rhyme, and he knows in general terms what will come next (if he can remember the rhyme), but he is kept guessing as to just how the author and the murderer will make the crime fit the rhyme. The most famous example of a nursery rhyme followed to the last detail is of course *Ten Little Niggers,* published in America variously as *And Then There Were None* and *Ten Little Indians,* in order to avoid any sense of prejudice. Naturally, in England, where people of the Negro race had up until the 1960's been so rare as to be curiosities, no one would have thought that using the word "niggers" in a children's rhyme would suggest any sense of prejudice or condemnation. The substitution made by Dodd, Mead of "Indians" for "niggers" was an inspiration in itself, for American Indians are held in a sense of curious respect by Americans, who both value them as a national treasure and are somewhat guilty in their minds about the more unpleasant results of the nineteenth century's Manifest Destiny, which simply took land away from the Indians. However, this substitution created a difficulty. As anyone who has ever traced, or tried to trace, nursery rhyme tunes knows, there are almost as many differing versions of tunes as there are people singing them. Appendix G gives tunes for the nursery rhymes Mrs. Christie has used, and she has kindly checked over the tunes to see that they are as she had them in mind while writing.

However, the English nursery rhyme "Ten Little

Niggers" appears never to have had a tune, and you will recall that in both the novel and play the tune was recited, not sung. In America, however, there is a nursery rhyme, with tune, which counts both up and down, and it is called "Ten Little Indians." The two appear to be completely unrelated, although those who wish to sing the English rhyme to the American tune can of course do so, as did Fabian in the 1965 film version of the story.

To settle the confusion once for all, both rhymes are printed below. The tune for the American rhyme is given in the Appendix, with indications for which quarter notes (crotchets) to divide to make the American tune fit the totally unrelated English rhyme, if desired. English counting-out rhyme, as used by Agatha Christie in *Ten Little Niggers:*

Ten little nigger boys going out to dine,
One choked his little self, and then there were nine.
Nine little nigger boys sat up very late,
One overslept himself, and then there were eight.
Eight little nigger boys going down to Devon,
One got left behind, and then there were seven.
Seven little nigger boys chopping up sticks,
One chopped himself in half, and then there were six.
Six little nigger boys playing with a hive,
A bumblebee stung one, and then there were five.
Five little nigger boys going in for law,
One got in Chancery, and then there were four.
Four little nigger boys sailing out to sea,
A red herring swallowed one, and then there were three.
Three little nigger boys going to the Zoo,
A big bear hugged one, and then there were two.
Two little nigger boys sitting in the sun,

One got frizzled up, and then there was one.
One little nigger boy left all alone,
He went and hanged himself, and then there were none.

And the American rhyme:

> One little, two little, three little Indians,
> Four little, five little, six little Indians,
> Seven little, eight little, nine little Indians,
> Ten little Indian boys. And there were:
> Ten little, nine little, eight little Indians,
> Seven little, six little, five litttle Indians,
> Four little, three little, two little Indians,
> One little Indian boy.

The most that can be said in favour of that latter rhyme is that it is inane in the extreme. But it does have a good tune. However, the English rhyme has yet another interesting facet, as Mrs. Christie tells us. " 'He went and hanged himself' is, I am fairly sure, the original ending, but 'He got married, and then there were none' was going in my childhood days." And Mrs. Christie used the original ending in the novel, and the newer "He got married" ending in the play, rewriting her most ingenious plot so that it would better fit the conventions of drama, and it is a tribute to her imagination that both endings work out convincingly.

Other favourite nursery rhymes of Mrs. Christie's evidently include "Sing a Song of Sixpence," which has been used in the short story of that name from *The Listerdale Mystery,* very prominently in the full-length novel *A Pocket Full of Rye,* and also in the short story "Four and Twenty Blackbirds" from

The Adventure of the Christmas Pudding and Other Stories. "How does your garden grow?" provided a unifying theme for the story of the same name in *The Regatta Mystery.* "One, two, buckle my shoe" was followed religiously in the novel of the same title, called *The Patriotic Murders* in America. "Five Little Pigs" suggested the inspiration for the Poirot novel which was later made into a very successful play—as usual, the English title of the book is the same as that of the rhyme. One of Mrs. Christie's own special favourites is *Crooked House,* which she says she "saved up for years, thinking about it, working it out. I don't (she continues) know what put the Leonides family into my head—they just came. I feel that I myself was only their scribe." It is the fact that the family is unusual and special, rather than "crooked," that evidently inspired the author. *Hickory, Dickory, Dock* (1955) is the most recent full-length novel using a nursery rhyme as its theme.

However, a certain Mother Goose book played an important role in *N or M?* (1941), and who will ever forget the fury and frustration of the German plotter when Tuppence, in answer to a threat, chirps out "Goosey, goosey, gander!" in the same book?

Mrs. Christie knows her Bible and her Shakespeare, as *The Pale Horse,* with its title taken from Revelation, and *There Is a Tide* (*Julius Caesar,* IV, iii) demonstrate. "The Mousetrap," Mrs. Christie admits with a smile, was in fact written to supply the play Hamlet had in mind but never got around to seeing performed in full:

King Claudius: What do you call the play?
Hamlet: The Mouse-trap . . . 'Tis a knavish piece of
work: but what of that?

[*Hamlet,* III, ii, 40-43]

And it is perhaps a piece of poetic justice that the
most famous play in the English language should have
supplied the title for the longest-running play in
England.

Mrs. Christie's interest in spiritualism is evidently
quite an old one, for séances and table-tapping appear fairly often in her books. *The Hound of Death*
short story collection contains quite a few stories
which are not detection at all, but rather pure fantasy.
In her 1956 interview with Nigel Dennis, Mrs.
Christie expressed a keen interest in science fiction,
but it is worth noting that in the intervening decade
she has avoided both science fiction and fantasy as
main themes. She has rather made spiritualism a
cover or camouflage for straight mystery and detection, although one at times wonders in *The Pale
Horse* if it is possible to commit murder by telepathy.
But the presence of Mrs. Christie's humorous alter-
ego, Mrs. Ariadne Oliver, should tip the reader off,
for that lady detective writer has been known to
utter casual phrases in early chapters which later turn
out to have been quite prophetic.

Related to this kind of fantasy is Mrs. Christie's
extreme fondness for that sort of Guignol show
known as the Harlequinade, and her poetry collection of the 1920's, *Road of Dreams,* has a poem quite
extended in length in which Mrs. Christie details the

characters and puts on a harlequin show of her own. Mr. Harley Quin, who keeps inspiring Mr. Satterthwaite in *The Mysterious Mr. Quin* short stories, is definitely this same motley-coloured gentleman of supernatural knowledge—although one at times wonders if he is the personification of Death as well. But as Mr. Satterthwaite reappears later in *Three-Act Tragedy,* we are probably justified in concluding not, for in that later book Mr. Satterthwaite casually mentions his acquaintance with Mr. Quin by referring obliquely to the short story "At the Bells and Motley."

Mrs. Christie says that she would like to try her hand at other than detective stories and novels, and she has written some straight novels under the name of Mary Westmacott, some poems and short stories of a Christmas nature under the name Agatha Christie Mallowan, and the aforementioned autobiographical *Come, Tell Me How You Live* under the Mallowan name as well. These works are all catalogued in Appendix A of this book for the reader who wishes to pursue them. However, curiously enough, like Mary Roberts Rinehart, Mrs. Christie's talents seem most aptly used in the detective story—her talents are analytical, wryly humorous, and penetrating in telling a tightly-knit story, and her romance always seems less convincing. Perhaps this is due to the fact that the detective story and novel are essentially a cerebral form, thanks to their conventions and confines of plot, and the sort of mind who likes well-made plots is not likely to go in for formless romance and affection as well—murder (in fiction, at least) conforms to disciplines that love does not.

For instance, it would be very hard to imagine either Miss Jane Marple or M. Hercule Poirot falling madly and wildly in love. The mere suggestion that Poirot might be amorously attracted to the Countess Rossakoff caused Miss Lemon to forget her filing system in *The Labours of Hercules*! And Miss Marple is too busy wondering what everyone else is doing to have affairs of her own. Both of these sleuths derive their satisfaction from life by vicarious means, as we shall see in the next two chapters.

CHAPTER FIVE

M. Hercule Poirot

ERLE STANLEY GARDNER was once written to by an irate reader who noted that in the course of ten years Della Street's eyes had changed colour, and Perry Mason and Paul Drake had moved their offices without ever bothering to inform the reading public. Mr. Gardner, rising to the challenge, wrote back (and published the reply) to say that Della's eyes looked blue or green, depending upon which light you saw them in, and that the office move had been made (as I recall) at the request of the building's owner during those war years when there were supposed to be waiting lists for better apartments and offices, and Mason and his detective were being accorded special preference.

To a certain extent, Agatha Christie admits, she has been plagued with the same sort of problem, for Poirot very clearly retired in 1904—*The Mysterious Affair at Styles* unequivocally said so in 1920. At that time neither Poirot nor his creator ever expected a distinguished career-in-retirement of fifty years for the Belgian. And Mrs. Christie has simply given up trying to make Poirot older as the years go by, agreeing finally that Poirot and Miss Marple both exist in that eternal summer of which Shakespeare speaks in the sonnet, although eternal autumn might be a better image.

For Poirot does represent wisdom, experience, and the tolerance which comes with age. He is finicky, to be sure, but how often has he arranged little matches, love affairs, and career opportunities at the end of books for young people who have had the misfortune to have a brush with murder. *Death in the Clouds, Murder on the Links,* and *One, Two, Buckle My Shoe* are but three examples of such matchmaking, or at least lively interest in the future of young people with marital intentions.

Poirot stands for tradition, for order and method for its own sake. In a world beset with confusion, disagreement, and strife, he is always calm and collected, and resassures us that reason can resolve any problem or complexity. He generally supports the English idea of justice; in fact, this author can think of only two instances in which his actions could be called even questionable. In *Murder on the Orient Express,* Poirot's "solution" is prompted by the fact that American justice has been patently lax in punishing the guilty—and Mrs. Christie's attitude towards Americans during the 1920's and 1930's represents an interesting caricature of the way Americans were seen by Europeans at the time. Evidently they spent all their time saying, as Jonathan Miller put it, "Aw.

gee! I guess you're just plumb crazy!" when they could be dissuaded from letting their revolvers do their talking for them. It was probably Mrs. Christie's sense of humour which permitted her to keep her very considerable American following during those years.

Poirot's appearance has been detailed so many times that it seems scarcely necessary to do more than mention it briefly here. He is precisely five feet four inches tall. His head is egg-shaped, and he carries it a little to the left (what lack of order and method!). His eyes shine green when he is excited, and he still wears black patent leather shoes, although in recent years he has given up carrying a cane, owing, perhaps, to the fact that he has recovered from the injury which made him limp in 1920. His moustaches are twirled ferociously into points at the end, and he uses a certain "tonic, not a dye" to keep his hair a suspiciously young-looking colour.

He lived originally in London at 14, Farraway Street with Captain Hastings, his Watson, but moved in the early 1930's to Whitehaven Mansions, a then modern block of flats which he chose because of their strictly goemetrical appearance and proportions. His valet for many years was Georges, who was previously in the service of Lord Edward Frampton. Poirot laments the fact that Georges' brain was strictly English (a synonym, we presume Poirot means, for "dense"), but Poirot never ceased to marvel at the quiet efficiency of the servant who would keep such things as beer in the flat for those occasions when Inspector Japp would pop in.

Poirot's English used to be deliberately abominable, because he realised that the English as a nation could be tricked into saying things if only a foreigner was around, and his bad English added the touch which his slightly comic appearance lacked. Anyone who looked as he looked and spoke as he spoke could be nothing but a mountebank, Poirot shrewdly figured that Englishmen would conclude. Yet notice how in the last chapter Poirot's English suddenly becomes idiomatic. When taxed with this fact, Poirot admitted to the knowledge of better English than he often spoke, and gave this as the reason for such atrocities as "Do not derange yourself, I pray you, monsieur."

When one compares an early short story collection such as *Poirot Investigates* (1924) with a recent book such as *The Clocks* (1963), one sees that fame has made a change in Poirot. For one thing, it used to be obligatory in the world of detective fiction for all the major characters, including the detective, to be presented by the close of the first chapter. Now, as Mrs. Christie readily admits, "you hold off Poirot as long as you can." This is smart psychology. For one thing, it permits youngsters such as Colin Lamb to have a go at solving the problem at hand themselves before they call in Poirot. Then, when they are all at sea, they call in the elderly expert, who works almost from his armchair to solve the problem.

But not quite. Poirot, fortunately, is not altogether predictable. We mentioned two instances in which his solution of a problem was not quite *comme il faut.* The first, *Murder on the Orient Express,* we have discussed. The second occurs in "The (Mystery of the) Chocolate Box" from *Poirot Investigates.* You will notice that in this case Poirot defers to two authorities even older than himself—motherhood and the Roman Catholic Church. It would be unkind to ask Mrs. Christie (like that uppity reader of Erle Stanley Gardner's) why Poirot, if he is so *bon catholique,* does not attend Mass, and so we shall refrain. Actually, the only church service this author can remember his attending was Anglican Matins (Morning Prayer) in *One, Two, Buckle My Shoe,* and he apparently got something out of it, for his hesitant baritone which quavered in Psalm 140, as he joined the congregation in the Anglican chant, suggested to him that he had in fact fallen into the snare which the proud had laid for him (verse 5), and the First Lesson (Samuel 15) stayed with him until the last chapter of the book. Incidentally, thanks to the English custom of singing the entire 150 Psalms of David each month, it is possible to date with some accuracy M. Poirot's visit to Alistair Blunt's country house in Kent. As Poirot went to church on a Sunday morning, and as the 140th Psalm is to be sung on the morning of the twenty-ninth day of the month, and further, as *One, Two, Buckle My Shoe* was delivered to the printers early in 1940, one can, by using his little grey cells (and a perpetual calendar), discern clearly that Poirot's visit to Kent occurred on either Sunday, 29 January 1939, or Sunday, 29 October 1939, with the latter date the more likely, as Poirot refrains from adverse comments upon the weather.

Agatha Christie has admitted that her books employ a good deal more sitting around and theorising than they do running about "like the foxhound, with his nose to the ground," to quote Poirot's opinion of the arrogant French detective Giraud whom he bested in *The Murder on the Links*. In fact, movie producers have used this argument as basis for changing plots and adding such things as a stable full of horses (Murder at the Gallop), the film which took Poirot out of the story *After the Funeral,* added Miss Marple, and then put her on a horse. "Quite unthinkable!" said Nora Blackborow, secretary to Mrs. Christie's agents, "Miss Marple on a—horse!" Perhaps Sherlock Holmes is not the only detective whose followers believe the image cannot be tampered with, and perhaps the thing which has deterred the founding of a Christie fan club is the fact that readers' fondness seems to be equally divided between Hercule Poirot and Miss Marple, who have very little in common, save for the fact that they both think clearly.

It is not, however, precisely true to say Hercule Poirot is completely cerebral. For instance, his inquisitive instincts lead him to the scene of the crime a good deal of the time, in spite of the fact that he says human bloodhounds can bring him clues. Furthermore, for someone who thinks so clearly, it is amazing how often he is able to catch our excitement at the end with "Epatant! I am a triple imbecile, a thousand fools! If only we are not too late! Quick, Hastings!" And off he rushes, arriving just in the nick of time to prevent another murder. In fact, old Hercule is borrowing from the American Western films—this is his version of The Chase.

When one stops to think of how many times Poirot fans and Christie readers have swallowed this hoary device without choking, it is amazing. This is not to say by any means that the convention is inappropriate or second-rate, for it is no more stilted than the *deus ex machina* of Greek drama, for instance, and the fact that we know what the outcome will eventually be appeals to the child in all of us, as well as to the yearning for order and method in a confused world. The way Mrs. Christie brings it off is to make us feel each time that Poirot's egotism is about to catch up with him and undo him—the hero is about to be undone by his tragic flaw. Yet as the detective story is always a comedy in the strict and literary sense of the word, this has not yet happened, but this commentator is not so foolish as to go out on a limb and say that anything is beyond Mrs. Christie. She would, undoubtedly, accept it as a challenge, and all the changes have not been rung on the detective story format by a long chalk, Dorothy Sayers' *The Nine Tailors* to the contrary.

Mrs. Christie at one time grew tired of her little Belgian, whose phrase "the little grey cells" has been adopted by an African tribe to indicate their brain. However, the English language's second most-translated author (Shakespeare is the first on the list) seems to have abandoned her plan to put Poirot into a wheelchair, fortunately, and has accepted him as one of the unchanging facts of English life, like the monarchy and the Prayer Book. It is good to have some unchanging things in an unsettled world.

The following is a list of all the books in which Poirot appears, in chronological order. The titles, when variants exist, are the original English ones, and the dates of publication are those of the first English editions of the works. Appendix B will easily cross-reference American variants of these English titles.

Mysterious Affair at Styles (1920)
Murder on the Links (1923)
Poirot Investigates (1924)
Murder of Roger Ackroyd (1926)
The Big Four (1927)
Mystery of the Blue Train (1928)
Peril at End House (1932)
Lord Edgware Dies (1933)
Murder on the Orient Express (1934)
Three-Act Tragedy (1935)
The A.B.C. Murders (1935)
Death in the Clouds (1935)
Murder in Mesopotamia (1936)
Cards on the Table (1936)
Dumb Witness (1937)
Death on the Nile (1937)
Murder in the Mews (1937)
Appointment with Death (1938)

Hercule Poirot's Christmas (1938)

The Regatta Mystery and Other Stories (1939)
(American only)

Sad Cypress (1940)

One, Two, Buckle My Shoe (1940)

Evil Under the Sun (1941)

Five Little Pigs (1943)

The Hollow (1946)

The Labours of Hercules (1947)

Taken at the Flood (1948)

Witness for the Prosecution and Other Stories
(1948) (American only)

Three Blind Mice and Other Stories (1950)
(American only)

The Under Dog and Other Stories (1951)
(American only)

Mrs. McGinty's Dead (1952)

After the Funeral (1953)

Hickory, Dickory, Dock (1955)

Dead Man's Folly (1956)

Cat Among the Pigeons (1959)

*Adventure of the Christmas Pudding and Other
Stories* (1960)

Double Sin and Other Stories (1961)
(American only)

The Clocks (1963)

Third Girl (1966)

CHAPTER SIX

Miss Jane Marple

MISS JANE MARPLE provides a good foil for Hercule Poirot. According to Mrs. Christie, "Miss Marple has some faint affinity with my own grandmother, also a pink and white old lady who, although having led the most sheltered and Victorian of lives, nevertheless always appeared to be intimately acquainted with the depths of human depravity. One could be made to feel incredibly naive and credulous by her reproachful remark: 'But did you believe what they said to you? I never do!' "

Mrs. Christie, in the introduction to one of the Penguin reprints of her books, goes on, "I enjoyed writing the Miss Marple stories *(The Thirteen Problems)* very much, conceived a great affection for my fluffy old lady, and hoped that she might be a success. She was. After the first six stories had appeared (in serial form) six more were requested. I think that she is her best in the solving of short problems; these thirteen problems (American title *The Tuesday*

Club Murders) I consider the real essence of Miss Marple for those who like her."

Miss Marple, tall and thin, with china blue eyes, used to wear a lace fichu and gloves. However, that was in 1928, and although she has perhaps aged twenty years in the intervening forty, she has kept up with fashions for older people. Although Mrs. Christie insists (often with indignation) that she does not model her characters after anyone living, *At Bertram's Hotel* (1965) shows a Miss Marple of about Mrs. Christie's age at the time: one who does not like walking too far on any one occasion, and one who would like to see an earlier England and its quiet, refined ways, but realises that she must move with the years. For one thing, this latest book is one of the first which shows Miss Marple thinking a great deal by herself—we see a great deal more of what goes on in Miss Marple's mind in *At Bertram's Hotel* than we used to in earlier books, wherein someone else told the story, and presented his or her views of Miss Marple. Furthermore, the earlier portraits of Miss Marple were considerably less flattering, as a comparison of *Bertram's* and the first full-length Miss Marple, *Murder at the Vicarage*, will easily show.

Although Miss Marple and Hercule Poirot both represent the wisdom of experience and long life, their methods of solving crime are different. Poirot treats each case with order and method, and regards it as unique, although he admits to having met some personality types, such as the gold-digging young woman, before. Miss Marple, on the other hand, solves every crime by analogy, for she insists that human nature never changes, which truism she proceeds to demonstrate by showng how the greengrocer's assistant jilted his girl in precisely the same way that the movie star has just done with his international beauty queen.

Some of all this talk, to be sure, is camouflage, and is intended as such. Miss Marple, by virtue of her sex and station, is forced to play a more confined role than Poirot, and often she sorts out the facts and gives the solution while she is knitting: a neat combination of The Old Man in the Corner and Madame Defarge. She readily admits to having knowledge her readers are not certain to possess, which in a certain sense is not playing fair, but she responds in a spirited fashion by admonishing her novelist nephew and man of the world Raymond West that her knowledge is plain and home-grown, just the product of life in a country village. In fact, the knowledge she possesses is easily found in a dictionary, gardening catalogue, or encyclopaedia, if one had the common sense to know what he should be looking up. For example, how many modern readers know that

> Rosemary is for remembrance,
> A yellow tulip means hopeless love,
> Orchids mean "I await your favours,"
> Dahlias mean treachery and misrepresentation.

If they know the first line quoted, they may consider themselves lucky, for spices and their "meanings" seem to have survived more than the floral connotations quoted. Yet the lines can be found in a library as easily as the dates on a perpetual calendar, or the rhyme beginning "Monday's child is fair of face," about equally misquoted. It would be rather fun to see what Miss Marple and Mrs. Christie could make of that latter Scottish rhyme.

As to the future of Miss Marple, it is hard to guess. She has grown frailer in recent years, and cannot garden as much as she once liked. But she still has her house in the village of St. Mary Mead, but the village is changing, as *The Mirror Crack'd* details. Yet she still is quite able to get around, and her mind is as sharp as ever. She has changed from a very shrewd small village pussy to a rather tolerant grand-mother type looking over the world, and in this sense, like Poirot, she has mellowed. She still sees wicked-ness, but has put away her bird glasses and depends more and more upon her insight. Rather than seek-ing out other people's transgressions, she now finds them literally forced upon her, even on a holiday in the Caribbean. Yet she still remains the English gentlewoman, and may well be the twentieth cen-tury's most famous example of the breed.

Miss Marple has appeared to date in the following books. As in the case of the Poirot titles, these are arranged chronologically. The titles and dates of publication are in all cases the English ones.

Murder at the Vicarage (1930)
The Thirteen Problems (1932)
The Regatta Mystery and Other Stories (1939)
(American only)

The Body in the Library (1942)
The Moving Finger (1943)
Three Blind Mice and Other Stories (1950)
(American only)
A Murder Is Announced (1950)
They Do It with Mirrors (1952)
A Pocket Full of Rye (1953)
4:50 from Paddington (1957)
Adventure of the Christmas Pudding and Other Stories (1960)
Double Sin and Other Stories (1961)
(American only)
The Mirror Crack'd from Side to Side (1962)
A Caribbean Mystery (1964)
At Bertram's Hotel (1965)

CHAPTER SEVEN

The A.B.C. Murders:
a Mystery Unravelled

IN THIS CHAPTER we plan to commit heresy and discuss a Christie novel in detail, giving away the ending at the beginning so that we may see in detail how Mrs. Christie goes to work in planting her clues, true and false. In other words, we shall discuss *The A.B.C. Murders* as though it were a straight novel. The choice of this one particular "vintage" Christie is not a random one. The book comes from her most prolific period—1934 saw the publication of no fewer than four Christies in the same year, and 1935 followed with *Three-Act Tragedy* and *The A.B.C. Murders*. One fascinating study is the interrelationship of the books during this period; for instance, *Three-Act Tragedy* and *A.B.C.* share a device of plot, and 1936's second book, *Cards on the Table*, seems to have been inspired by a remark at the end of Chapter III of *A.B.C.* To be more specific would be to "spoil" the books for the new Christie fan, but for those readers who are already familiar with all the plots in question, the search for interrelating clues will prove rewarding and fascinating.

The new Christie fan, or the reader who has not read *The A.B.C. Murders* recently enough to remember the plot in detail, is hereby advised to skip to the next chapter until that assignment has been completed, for if he turns the next page, he will find out whodunit.

The A.B.C. Murders derives its inspiration from that offhand remark of Chesterton's Father Brown—"Where to hide a tree but in a forest? Where to hide a cross but in a sea (see?) of crosses?" And Mrs. Christie thought, "Where to hide a murder but in a group of murders which appear to be connected, but which have nothing to do with each other save that the first one or two are committed to create atmosphere and background, and to provide an implied connexion.* The murder of importance will be murder number three."

This, one might say, was the basic inspiration behind the book. But now the plot needed additional false clues and refinements, which Mrs. Christie provided by having the murderer announce his crimes in advance by letter to Hercule Poirot. So far, the basic plot has been laid, but the gimmicks, the false clues still remain to be added. The British Railways Guide is called *The A.B.C. Guide,* and this set of initials suggested to Mrs. Christie an alphabetical sequence of crimes.

* Readers will also recall Poe's *Purloined Letters.*

Accordingly if Franklin Clarke is to be the murderer, and his brother, Sir Carmichael Clarke, the victim, it would be well for the victim to live in Churston. All that would then remain would be to provide a first victim with the initials A.A. who lived in a town beginning with A, and a second victim whose initials were B.B. and who lived in a town with a name in the B's, and the police should conclude (along with the readers) that a lunatic with an alphabetical complex (or at least a tabular mind) was at work. They should be kept so busy trying to find connexions between the murders that they would overlook the obvious and important point—Franklin Clarke needed and wanted money. But he had no interest in Mrs. Ascher from Andover nor in Betty Barnard from Bexhill-on-Sea. They were simply victims he eliminated in cold blood when the time came, placing an open copy of *The A.B.C. Guide* face downwards on the body, and, as a macabre touch, he opened the *Guide* to the listing of the town of that latest murder.

All of this planning had to go on in Franklin Clarke's head before he made a move, of course, and he was cunning enough to provide a scapegoat in case things should ever get too warm for him. He had met a man by the ludicrous name of Alexander Bonaparte Cust, and this poor wretch suffered from blackouts and epileptic seizures. All of his life he had been picked upon, and he felt that the world would always get the better of him. It was a simple matter for Franklin Clarke to urge the man to apply for a salesman's job in answer to a newspaper advertisement which Clarke had craftily placed. Needless to say, Cust was hired to show samples of ladies' stockings, and his unknown employer took pains to send Cust to Andover, Bexhill, and Churston on the days when murders were committed in those towns. Poor Cust actually ended up believing himself responsible for the murders, after the newspapers gave the sensational cases much publicity.

This advance planning would be enough for most writers, but Mrs. Christie is careful to take pains to lay still more false clues. She suggests that only the police know of the letters which Poirot gets before each crime, mentioning the location of the next murder. Therefore, are the police possibly implicated in the crimes? And she assigns an Inspector Crome to the case to further the suspicion which the reader soon develops about anyone even remotely connected with early letters of the alphabet. Clarke is smart enough to attempt a fourth murder, that of a Mr. Downes, although his aim is hampered by the darkened cinema house and he mistakes a Mr. Earlsfield for Downes.

This much of the plot must have been carefully worked out in the author's head before she began to write, for this much is necessary to tell the story forwards. Now for the unravelling. Where shall we make our murderer commit the mistakes which will lead Poirot to the correct solution? Cust, quite by the sort of natural accident which occurs in real life, happens to have a weak sort of alibi for the night of the Bexhill murder, although the police are ready to prove a case by any of the other three in the series, for it is only necessary to prove a man guilty of one murder to hang him, and thus get the newspapers off their hue and cry. This would have worked, for Franklin Clarke was smart enough to know when to stop. He was, as Poirot tells us repeatedly from the beginning, "a sane man," and the letters were the work of a sane man.

Obviously, this is a cool and collected story which would not lend itself to one of Poirot's famous chases-to-prevent-another-murder, and the haphazard selection of victims makes the idea of a baited trap using a decoy of the proper initials unworkable. Poirot then must rely on the explanatory last chapter with a trick to catch the criminal and make him admit his guilt. Chapter 34, "Poirot Explains," is a classic example of the confrontation scene in which the murderer is unmasked, usually with a little naughty trickery on Poirot's part—in this case the use of a pickpocket to keep Franklin Clarke from committing suicide when he admits his crime. Poirot details the little slips—the fingerprint on the typewriter, the witnesses who were able to identify Franklin Clarke, and so forth, that came to light once Poirot knew which man to suspect. But for the length of the book, Poirot has been reduced to trying to find clues in the letters themselves, which he is able to do to a certain extent—the letter writer's slight anti-foreign bias is also noticeable in Franklin Clarke. The only thing that remains is for Poirot to play Cupid, and unite two former suspects—Donald and Megan.

The story, when told forwards thus, sounds rather simple-minded and inane, not to say contrived. It is cerebral, and is as much an artificial exercise as the sonnet. But to criticise the detective story because of this is to miss an important fact of literary life—the detective story is not told forwards (until briefly, in the recapitulation); it is told backwards, as Sherlock Holmes kept insisting, and this simple and oft ignored fact of life is the gimmick or device which makes the form succeed.

As we have mentioned, in second-rate detective stories, the unravelling of the plot is the entire interest, and we must remember that early examples in any literary form are apt to be creaky and crude. Yet the better examples of the genre in its first century and a quarter are usually distinguished by the telling caricatures, and by the doubletalk of false clues which make the second reading more enjoyable than the first, for the second time round one can admire the author's techniques.

For this reason, it is perhaps a good idea to read the first chapter and then the last chapter of any Christie you've read some time ago, and whose outcome you remember.

By this process you familiarise yourself at the start with the names of the characters to watch, and you will appreciate as you go along (instead of later) remarks such as "I did all that needed to be done," or

"My dear girl, you can't possibly guess what's going through my mind at this moment!" Yet notice how casually and subtilely these clues are camouflaged in conversation. It is a fascinating study.

People have been complaining probably since the time of Poe that all the gimmicks and plots have been used up. This may or may not be true, but as the detective story enters its second quarter of its second century, skilled practitioners are finding new complexities that are still within the grasp of the average reader. For instance, in one of the books most alluded to in this work, *The Clocks* (1963), Mrs. Christie combines two plots in one, and winds them together at the end. This technique, of course, did not originate with the detective story, and perhaps its best practitioner in England was Thackeray, in the nineteenth century. If the detective story moves in this direction of cerebral complexity and unity instead of the direction of gadgetry, it should be able to survive for quite a while longer.

In an earlier chapter we alluded to the problem of imitation and inspiration as opposed to plagiarism. With the demand for detective fiction, it gets harder and harder with each passing year for an author to think up a situation or a device that has not been used at least once before. *The A.B.C. Murders,* after all, owed something to Chesterton. But two more recent books owe something more than inspiration to *The A.B.C. Murders.*

A lady in California who ought to have known better decided in the early 1960's that it was time some criminals tried a crime based on a classic detective novel. On the theory that the unkindest review we can give the book is not to mention its author and title, we shall simply state that the book featured two homosexuals caught in illegal actions. One of the pair happened to be a Christie fan and decided to put the plot of *The A.B.C. Murders* into action, committing two murders in order to mask the important third. Lacking an American equivalent to *The A.B.C. Guide,* they dumped California county guides on the bodies of their victims. The police detective assigned to the case made Hastings look brilliant by comparison—he had just moved, and had to unpack all his mystery novels before he could find the one with the plot he wanted. The extent of his deductive abilities, to make a long story mercifully short, consisted in recognising a matchbook from a homosexual night-club when it dropped out of the breast pocket of one of the gay pair.

That story, which added not one thing to the science of ratiocination, scarcely deserves the dignity of the name plagiarism. Prostitution might be a better literary term for that sort of swiping.

By happy contrast, *The Sleeping Car Murder* can be said to be an example of the reusing of a plot legitimately. This story is set in the 1960's, in Paris, and the locale and atmosphere add a good deal to the plot. Furthermore, one very vital change is made—the police now are involved in the story—a clue which was a red herring in the Christie story is now made of vital importance. One wishes that all post-O'Neill dramatists did not feel called upon to include sexual perversion (which, after all, is not a new phenomenon in the twentieth century, as Miss Marple would tell you), but *The Sleeping Car Murder* suggests much the same sort of relationship that the film *The Servant* did.

It is possible that the author of *The Sleeping Car Murder* had never read *A.B.C. Contre Poirot* as published in Paris by *Éditions du Masque* (Librairie des Champs-Élysées). For in spite of the fact that Mrs. Christie is translated even into Japanese, there are mystery writers who, undoubtedly, have not read all her books. Every how-to-do-it text on mystery writing urges neophytes to read widely in order to avoid coming up with a dashingly original plot which just happens, innocently, to use the Ackroyd gimmick, for instance.

Yet it will be hard for mystery writers of the last quarter of this century and all of the next not to be influenced one way or another by Agatha Christie, for she has proven herself prolific, facile—and perdurable.

CHAPTER EIGHT

Adaptations

THE ADAPTATION of Christie short stories and novels into plays and movies is documented in Appendix D and E, and that listing will answer the questions of who, when, and how.

Yet it would be remiss for us to conclude this little study of an author still very much alive and productive without some consideration of phenomena such as "The Mousetrap." Miss Marple has become vastly better known because of those movies starring Margaret Rutherford made in the 1960's than she ever was before, although of course the Miss Marple of the films and of the books are two quite separate entities. Unfortunately, it appears at this writing that no more Christie films will be made, for the film company which bought the rights to the Christie books possibly killed the goose that laid the golden egg. They put Miss Marple into Poirot books, and even produced a Miss Marple film with their own script, as if Mrs. Christie had not written enough suitable material. That particular film, "Murder Ahoy," did poorly when it came to reviews, and perhaps the 1965 version of "Ten Little Indians" and the film of *The A.B.C. Murders* ("The Alphabet Murders") may follow suit, thanks to their not having followed Christie more closely. It is a shame that we shall apparently have to speak of the moviemaking in a past tense for the moment, for with the almost unlimited number of Christie plots to draw on, films could be made at the rate of one a year for at least the next century.

However, she has said on more than one occasion that she feels *Witness for the Prosecution* to have been the best film adaptation of one of her works, and certainly the original version of *Ten Little Niggers*, released in America in 1945 under the title "And Then There Were None," kept much of the spirit of shock which the novel and the play communicated: that first version sagely kept all the people English and kept the time in the early 40's. The 1965 film remake was an international affair laid in Germany, and gathered together a jet set of cast with nothing in common except that all ten, incredibly enough in 1965, had not heard of that Agatha Christie mystery in which people were trapped on an island with a homicidal maniac. It would be an interesting latter-day psychological experiment to see if ten adults, chosen at random from reasonably good educational and financial backgrounds, could be found who did not possess at least one of their number who had some vague knowledge of that plot.

The most famous adaptation was made by Agatha Christie herself, and in fact she prefers to do her own adaptations for the stage. Hughes Massie Ltd, Mrs. Christie's agents, were approached one day by the BBC to see if Mrs. Christie might be able to do a radio play for, as Hamlet would have said, "a need." Suspecting that some sort of royal command performance might be in the offing (which no Englishman would refuse), Edmund Cork, Mrs. Christie's agent and friend of many years, found out that indeed Mrs. Christie would be able to supply a radio play. The request produced "The Mousetrap," a radio play for the eightieth birthday of Queen Mary, who had been approached by the BBC and asked what sort of programme she'd like. One of the things she fancied was a radio play by Agatha Christie.

The play found royal favour, and Mrs. Christie thereupon adapted it in two ways—into a short story, and into a stage play. Peter Saunders, the London producer, brought it to London to the Ambassadors Theatre in 1952 for a short run before releasing it to the repertory companies. It is still running at the Ambassadors Theatre, as of mid-1967, and shows no signs of old age, except that most of the cast changes annually, and two sets of furniture have been worn out. As yet no children of original performers are in the cast, but the play has long since bettered all endurance records in the history of the London theatre.

Why? The question seems difficult to answer. Peter Saunders confesses that he doesn't know; other Christies have come and gone since in both the West End and in New York. Mr. Saunders says that most Christies are too wholesome (fancy murder being that!) for modern London theatre critics; otherwise, he'd produce some more. "The Mousetrap" actually does not stand up in quality to "Witness for the Prosecution." The late Sir Winston Churchill confessed that he guessed the plot quite early, but he was the terror of actors and theatregoers alike, as Richard Burton so colourfully narrated when asked to reminisce about his experiences in the role of Hamlet. Obviously, the play is now running on its longevity, but it is very difficult to argue with that sort of success. It just seems difficult to explain it.

One thing which the MGM Miss Marple movies of the mid-1960's did do was to capture the essence of Mrs. Christie's in-jokes and humour. For instance, in "Murder She Said," the book Miss Marple was reading as she fell asleep on the train was an Agatha Christie; the play which the travelling players put on in "Murder Most Foul" was Agatha Christie's "Murder She Said," and the director of the repertory solemnly assured the cast on opening night of a new hit that "This will run longer than 'The Mousetrap'!"

Such humour was not without precedent in the books. Mrs. Ariadne Oliver, as we have mentioned, satirises lady detective writers; and the young adventurers, Tommy and Tuppence Beresford parody Poirot in one of this author's favourite short stories: "The Man Who Was No. 16," which one takes to represent *The Big Four*—squared. This last story in *Partners in Crime* shows clearly that Mrs. Christie intends never to fall into the most deadly of all authors' traps—that of taking oneself and one's work too seriously.

She is not that sort of person. She enjoys good food and good travel, good conversation and good furniture. In an age of anxiety, she still remembers how to laugh and how to relax. In her communication of these qualities of life, perhaps, Agatha Christie does fulfil the demands of those who insist that literature have a purpose and communicate a Truth.

Which conclusion, as John Donne said many years ago, "makes us end, where we begun."

Appendices

How to use the following appendices: A, An, and The are disregarded when they form the beginning of a title; otherwise, they count as full words. Thus, to look up "The Adventure of the Christmas Pudding," look under "Adventure." There you will find that it is a short story included in the short story collection of the same name. You will find full particulars as to date and company of publication under that title in the short story index. The same holds true for novels, plays, and films.

One final word of caution. We have tried, in every case, to list each title under all the forms in which it has appeared. But if you do not find a title such as "The Mystery of the Clapham Cook" listed under "mystery," try "The Affair of the Clapham Cook," and "The Clapham Cook." Generally, the errant story will turn up in one of the three places

Appendix A—all Christie titles listed alphabetically

Appendix B—novels alphabetised under English title, with complete information as to publisher, date of publication, detective, plot résumé, and alternate titles.

Appendix C—short story collections listed by title. Contents listed, along with publisher, date of publication, detective, and alternate titles. List of short stories not published in America and not published in England.

Appendix D—plays listed by title, with date of dramatisation and dramatiser. Cross reference for plays taken from novels and short stories.

Appendix E—films listed by title, with cross reference to the novel, short story, or play from which they are drawn.

Appendix F—Titles Not Published in America or England

Appendix G—the nursery rhymes used in the Christie books.

All Christie Titles Alphabetised

All Christie titles listed alphabetically, with classification into one of the following categories:

Novel (Appendix B)
Short Story (Appendix C)
Play (Appendix D)
Film (Appendix E)

For further information, proceed to the index indicated in this list beside the title you are searching.

A

Absent in the Spring—1944 straight novel written under the name Westmacott

A.B.C. Murders—1935 Poirot novel

Accident—ss in *Listerdale Mystery,* and *Witness and Other Stories*

Adventure of Johnny Waverly—ss in *Three Blind Mice and Other Stories*

Adventure of the Cheap Flat—ss in *Poirot Investigates*

Adventure of the Christmas Pudding—1960 English ss collection

Adventure of the Christmas Pudding—ss in above collection

Adventure of the Clapham Cook—ss in *The Under Dog and Other Stories*

Adventure of the Egyptian Tomb—ss in *Poirot Investigates*

Adventure of the Italian Nobleman—ss in *Poirot Investigates*

Adventure of the King of Clubs——ss in *The Under Dog and Other Stories*

Adventure of the Sinister Stranger—ss in *Partners in Crime*

Adventure of the Western Star—ss in *Poirot Investigates*

Affair at the Bungalow—ss in *The Thirteen Problems*

Affair at the Victory Ball—ss in *The Under Dog and Other Stories*

Affair in the Flat—see A Fairy in the Flat

Affair of the Pink Pearl—ss in *Partners in Crime*

Affair of the Sinister Stranger—ss in *Partners in Crime*

After the Funeral—1953 Poirot novel

Afternoon at the Seaside—one-act play in *Rule of Three*

Alibi—1928 play based on *Murder of Roger Ackroyd*

Alphabet Murders—film based on *The A.B.C. Murders*

Ambassador's Boots—ss in *Partners in Crime*

And Then There Were None—see *Ten Little Niggers*

Apples of the Hesperides—ss in *The Labours of Hercules*

Appointment with Death—1938 Poirot novel

Appointment with Death—1945 play based on the above

Arcadian Deer—ss in *The Labours of Hercules*

At Bertram's Hotel—1965 Miss Marple novel

At the Bells and Motley—ss in *The Mysterious Mr. Quin*

Augean Stables—ss in *The Labours of Hercules*

B

Baited Trap—ss made over into novel chapter in *The Big Four*

Big Four—1927 Poirot novel, made over from sss

Bird with the Broken Wing—ss in *The Mysterious Mr Quin*

Black Coffee—1934 original play; film version under same title

Blindman's Buff—ss in *Partners in Crime*

Bloodstained Pavement—ss in *The Thirteen Problems*

Blue Geranium—ss in *The Thirteen Problems*
Body in the Library—1942 Miss Marple novel
Boomerang Clue—see *Why Didn't They Ask Evans?*
Burden, The—1956 straight novel pub. under the name West-
    macott
By Road or Rail—see Double Sin

C

Call of Wings—ss in *Hound of Death*
Capture of Cerberus—ss in *The Labours of Hercules*
Cards on the Table—1936 Poirot novel
Caribbean Mystery—1964 Miss Marple novel
Case of the Buried Treasure—see Strange Jest
Case of the Caretaker—ss in *Three Blind Mice and Other*
    Stories
Case of the City Clerk—ss in *Parker Pyne Investigates*
Case of the Discontented Husband—ss in *Parker Pyne Investi-*
    gates
Case of the Discontented Soldier—ss in *Parker Pyne Investi-*
    gates
Case of the Distressed Lady—ss in *Parker Pyne Investigates*
Case of the Middle-Aged Wife—ss in *Parker Pyne Investigates*
Case of the Missing Lady—ss in *Partners in Crime*
Case of the Missing Will—ss in *Poirot Investigates*
Case of the Perfect Maid—ss in *Three Blind Mice and Other*
    Stories
Case of the Retired Jeweller—see Tape-Measure Murder
Case of the Rich Woman—ss in *Parker Pyne Investigates*
Cat Among the Pigeons—1959 Poirot novel
Chess Problem—ss made over into novel chapter in 1927
    Poirot novel *The Big Four*
Chocolate Box—ss in *Poirot Investigates*
Christmas Tragedy—ss in *The Thirteen Problems*
Clergyman's Daughter—ss in *Partners in Crime*
Clocks—1963 Poirot novel
Come and Be Hanged—see *Towards Zero*

Come, Tell Me How You Live—1946 autobiographical account
  of archaeological trips pub. under the name Agatha
  Christie Mallowan
Coming of Mr. Quin—ss in *The Mysterious Mr. Quin*
Companion—ss in *The Thirteen Problems*
Cornish Mystery—ss in *The Under Dog and Other Stories*
Crackler—ss in *Partners in Crime*
Cretan Bull—ss in *The Labours of Hercules*
Crooked House—1949 novel

D

Daughter's a Daughter—1952 straight novel written under the
  name Westmacott
Dead Harlequin—ss in *The Mysterious Mr. Quin*
Dead Man's Folly—1956 Poirot novel
Dead Man's Mirror—American ss collection
Dead Man's Mirror—ss in *Murder in the Mews* and in Am.
  coll. *Dead Man's Mirror*
Death by Drowning—ss in *The Thirteen Problems*
Death Comes as the End—1945 novel
Death in the Air—see *Death in the Clouds*
Death in the Clouds—1935 Poirot novel
Death on the Nile—ss in *Parker Pyne Investigates*. No relation
  to novel or play of same title
Death on the Nile—1937 Poirot novel; 1946 play
Destination Unknown—1954 novel
Disappearance of Mr. Davenheim—ss in *Poirot Investigates*
Double Clue—ss in *Double Sin and Other Stories*
Double Sin—ss in Am. short story collection of same name.
  Original title of ss—By Road or Rail
Double Sin and Other Stories—American only ss collection
Dream—ss in *Adventure of the Christmas Pudding; The Re-
  gatta Mystery*
Dressmaker's Doll—ss in *Double Sin and Other Stories*
Dumb Witness—1937 Poirot novel
Dying Chinaman—ss made over into novel chapter in *The
  Big Four*

E

Easy to Kill—see Murder Is Easy
Erymanthian Boar—ss in *The Labours of Hercules*
Evil Under the Sun—1941 Poirot novel

F

Face of Helen—ss in *The Mysterious Mr. Quin*
Fairy in the Flat—ss in *Partners in Crime*
Finessing the King—ss in *Partners in Crime*
Five Little Pigs—1943 Poirot novel
Flock of Geryon—ss in *The Labours of Hercules*
Four and Twenty Blackbirds—ss in *Adventure of the Christmas Pudding; Three Blind Mice*
4:50 from Paddington—1957 Miss Marple novel
Four Suspects—ss in *The Thirteen Problems*
Fourth Man—ss in *Hound of Death; Witness for the Prosecution and Other Stories*
Fruitful Sunday—ss in *Listerdale Mystery*
Funerals Are Fatal—see *After the Funeral*

G

Gate of Baghdad—ss in *Parker Pyne Investigates*
Gentleman Dressed in Newspaper—ss in *Partners in Crime*
Giants' Bread—1930 straight novel pub. under the name Westmacott
Girdle of Hippolyta—ss in *The Labours of Hercules*
Girl in the Train—ss in *Listerdale Mystery*
Go Back for Murder—1960 play dramatised from 1943 Poirot novel *Five Little Pigs,* q.v.
Golden Ball—ss in *Listerdale Mystery*
Greenshaw's Folly—ss in *Adventure of the Christmas Pudding; Double Sin and Other Stories*
Gypsy—ss in *Hound of Death*

H

Hand Having Writ—see *The Moving Finger*

Harlequin's Lane—ss in *The Mysterious Mr. Quin*

Have You Got Everything You Want? ss in *Parker Pyne Investigates*

Herb of Death—ss in *The Thirteen Problems*

Hercule Poirot's Christmas—1938 Poirot novel

Hickory, Dickory, Death—see *Hickory, Dickory, Dock*

Hickory, Dickory, Dock—1955 Poirot novel

Hollow—1946 Poirot novel

Hollow—1951 play based on above

Horses of Diomedes—ss in *The Labours of Hercules*

Hound of Death—1933 ss collection, published in England only

Hound of Death—ss in collection of same name

House of Lurking Death—ss in *Partners in Crime*

House at Shiraz—ss in *Parker Pyne Investigates*

How Does Your Garden Grown?—ss in *Regatta Mystery*

How It All Came About— Foreword to *The Labours of Hercules*

I

Idol House of Astarte—ss in *The Thirteen Problems*

In a Glass Darkly—ss in *Regatta Mystery*

In the House of the Enemy—ss made over into novel chapter in *The Big Four*

Incredible Theft—ss in *Murder in the Mews*

Ingots of Gold—ss in *The Thirteen Problems*

J

Jane in Search of a Job—ss in *Listerdale Mystery*

Jewel Robbery at the Grand Metropolitan—ss in *Poirot Investigates*

K

Kidnapped Prime Minister—ss in *Poirot Investigates*

Kidnapping of Johnny Waverly—see The Adventure of Johnny Waverly

King of Clubs—see The Adventure of the King of Clubs

L

Labours of Hercules—1947 Poirot ss collection

Lady on the Stairs—see The Radium Thieves

Lamp—ss in *Hound of Death*

Last Séance—ss in *Hound of Death; Double Sin and Other Stories*

Lemesurier Inheritance—ss in *The Under Dog and Other Stories*

Lernean Hydra—ss in *The Labours of Hercules*

Listerdale Mystery—1934 ss collection, published in England only

Listerdale Mystery—ss in above collection

Lord Edgware Dies—1933 Poirot novel

Lost Mine—ss in *Poirot Investigates*

Love Detectives—ss in *Three Blind Mice and Other Stories*

Love from a Stranger—1936 play based on ss "Philomel Cottage"—also 2 film versions of same play with this title

M

Maid Who Disappeared—see Case of the Perfect Maid

Man from the Sea—ss in *The Mysterious Mr. Quin*

Man in the Brown Suit—1924 novel

Man in the Mist—ss in *Partners in Crime*

Man Who Was Number 16—ss in *Partners in Crime*

Manhood of Edward Robinson—ss in *Listerdale Mystery*

Market Basing Mystery—ss in *The Under Dog and Other Stories*

Million Dollar (Bond) Bank Robbery—ss in *Poirot Investigates*

Mirror Crack'd (from Side to Side)—1962 Miss Marple novel

Miss Marple Tells a Story—ss in *The Regatta Mystery*

Mr. Eastwood's Adventure—ss in *Listerdale Mystery;* also in Am. coll. *Witness and Other Stories* under title "Mystery of the Spanish Shawl"

Mr. Parker Pyne, Detective—see *Parker Pyne Investigates*

Mrs. McGinty's Dead—1952 Poirot novel

Motive vs Opportunity—ss in *The Thirteen Problems*

Mousetrap—1952 play, based on ss "Three Blind Mice"

Moving Finger—1943 Miss Marple novel

Murder After Hours—see *The Hollow*

Murder at Hazelmoor—see *The Sittaford Mystery*

Murder at Littlegreen House—see *Dumb Witness*

Murder at the Gallop—film based on *After the Funeral*

Murder at the Vicarage—1930 Miss Marple novel

Murder at the Vicarage—1950 play based on the above novel

Murder for Christmas—see *Hercule Poirot's Christmas*

Murder in Mesopotamia—1936 Poirot novel

Murder in Retrospect—see *Five Little Pigs*

Murder in the Calais Coach—see *Murder on the Orient Express*

Murder in the Mews—1937 Poirot ss collection

Murder in the Mews—ss in above collection

Murder in Three Acts—see *Three-Act Tragedy*

Murder Is Announced—1950 Miss Marple novel

Murder Is Easy—1939 novel

Murder Most Foul—film based on *Mrs. McGinty's Dead*

Murder of Roger Ackroyd—1926 Poirot novel

Murder on the Links—1923 Poirot novel

Murder on the Nile—1946 play based on novel *Death on the Nile,* not on ss Death on the Nile

Murder on the Orient Express—1934 Poirot novel

Murder She Said—film based on *4:50 from Paddington*

Murder with Mirrors—1952 Miss Marple novel

Mysterious Affair at Styles—1920 Poirot novel

Mysterious Mr. Quin—1930 ss collection featuring Mr. Satterthwaite

Mystery at Littlegreen House—see *Dumb Witness*

Mystery of the Baghdad Chest—ss in *The Regatta Mystery*. See also Mystery of the Spanish Chest

Mystery of the Blue Jar—ss in *Hound of Death; Witness and Other Stories*

Mystery of the Blue Train—1928 Poirot novel

Mystery of Hunter's Lodge—ss in *Poirot Investigates*

Mystery of the Plymouth Express—ss in *The Under Dog and Other Stories*

Mystery of the Spanish Chest—ss in *Adventure of the Christmas Pudding*—expanded form of Mystery of the Baghdad Chest

Mystery of the Spanish Shawl—see Mr. Eastwood's Adventure

N

N or M?—1941 Tommy and Tuppence Beresford novel

Nemean Lion—ss in *The Labours of Hercules*

Nursery Rhyme Murders—see *Ten Little Niggers*

O

One, Two, Buckle My Shoe—1940 Poirot novel

Oracle at Delphi—ss in *Parker Pyne Investigates*

Ordeal by Innocence—1958 novel

Outraged Heart—see *The Hollow*

Overdose of Death—see *One, Two, Buckle My Shoe*

P

Pale Horse—1961 novel

Parker Pyne Investigates—1934 ss collection

Partners in Crime—1929 ss collection featuring Tommy and Tuppence Beresford

Passing of Mr. Quin—ss in *The Mysterious Mr. Quin*

Patient—one-act play in *Rule of Three*

Patriotic Murders—see *One, Two, Buckle My Shoe*

Pearl of Price—ss in *Parker Pyne Investigates*

Peril at End House—1932 Poirot novel

Peril at End House—1940 play based on the above novel

Peroxide Blonde—ss included in novel *The Big Four*
Philomel Cottage—ss in *Listerdale Mystery; Witness and Other Stories*
Plymouth Express—see Mystery of the Plymouth Express
Pocket Full of Rye—1953 Miss Marple novel
Poirot Indulges a Whim—see The Adventure of the Cheap Flat
Poirot Investigates—1924 Poirot ss collection
Poirot Loses a Client—see *Dumb Witness*
Pot of Tea—ss in *Partners in Crime*
Problem at Pollensa Bay—ss in *Regatta Mystery*
Problem at Sea—ss in *Regatta Mystery*

R

Radium Thieves—ss made over into novel chapter in *The Big Four*
Rajah's Emerald—ss in *Listerdale Mystery*
Rats—one-act play in *Rule of Three*
Red House—ss in *Partners in Crime*
Red Signal—ss in *Hound of Death; Witness and Other Stories*
Regatta Mystery—1939 ss collection
Regatta Mystery—ss in above collection
Remembered Death—see *Sparkling Cyanide*
Rose and the Yew Tree—1947 straight novel written under name of Westmacott
Rule of Three—1962 collection of three one-act plays

S

Sad Cypress—1940 Poirot novel
Sanctuary—ss in *Double Sin and Other Stories*
Second Gong—ss in *Witness and Other Stories*
Secret Adventure—see *N or M?*
Secret Adversary—1922 Tommy and Tuppence Beresford novel
Secret of Chimneys—1925 novel
Seven Dials Mystery—1929 novel

Shadow on the Glass—ss in *The Mysterious Mr. Quin*
Sign in the Sky—ss in *The Mysterious Mr. Quin*
Sing a Song of Sixpence—ss in *Listerdale Mystery*
Sittaford Mystery—1931 novel
So Many Steps to Death—see *Destination Unknown*
SOS—ss in *Hound of Death; Witness and Other Stories*
Soul of the Croupier—ss in *The Mysterious Mr. Quin*
Sparkling Cyanide—1945 novel
Spider's Web—1954 play; film version with same title
Star over Bethlehem—1965 non-mystery Christmas ss and poem
    collection under name Mallowan
Strange Case of Sir Arthur Carmichael—ss in *Hound of Death*
Strange Jest—ss in *Three Blind Mice and Other Stories*
Stymphalean Birds—ss in *The Labours of Hercules*
Submarine Plans—ss in *The Under Dog and Other Stories*
Sunningdale Mystery—ss in *Partners in Crime*
Swan Song—ss in *Listerdale Mystery*

T

Taken at the Flood—1948 Poirot novel
Tape-Measure Murder—ss in *Three Blind Mice and Other*
    Stories
Ten Little Indians—see *Ten Little Niggers*
Ten Little Niggers—1939 novel; dramatised, and made into 2
    film versions
Terrible Catastrophe—ss made over into novel chapter in *The*
    Big Four
Theft of the Royal Ruby—ss in *Double Sin and Other Stories*
    see also Adventure of the Christmas Pudding
There Is a Tide—see *Taken at the Flood*
They Came to Baghdad—1951 novel
They Do It with Mirrors—see *Murder with Mirrors*
Third Floor Flat—ss in *Three Blind Mice and Other Stories*
Third Girl—1966 Poirot novel
Thirteen at Dinner—see *Lord Edgware Dies*
13 For Luck—1961 ss collection featuring works published
    elsewhere

Thirteen Problems—1932 Miss Marple collection
Three-Act Tragedy—1935 Poirot novel
Three Blind Mice—1950 ss collection
Three Blind Mice—ss in above collection, see also The Mouse-trap
Thumb Mark of St. Peter—ss in *Thirteen Problems*
Towards Zero—1944 novel
Towards Zero—play dramatised from above novel
Tragedy at Marsdon Manor—ss in *Poirot Investigates*
Triangle at Rhodes—ss in *Murder in the Mews*
Tuesday Club Murders—see *Thirteen Problems*
Tuesday Night Club—ss in above collection

U

Unbreakable Alibi—ss in *Partners in Crime*
Under Dog and Other Stories—1952 Poirot ss collection
Under Dog—ss in above collection
Unexpected Guest—1958 play
Unexpected Guest—ss made over into novel chapter in *The Big Four*
Unfinished Portrait—1934 straight novel written under the name of Westmacott

V

Veiled Lady—ss in *Poirot Investigates*
Verdict—1958 play
Village Murder—see Tape-Measure Murder
Voice in the Dark—ss in *The Mysterious Mr. Quin*

W

Wasps' Nest—ss in *Double Sin and Other Stories*
What Mrs. McGillicuddy Saw!—see *4:50 from Paddington*
Why Didn't They Ask Evans?—1934 novel

Where There's a Will—see Wireless

Wireless—ss in *Hound of Death; Witness and Other Stories*

Witness for the Prosecution—ss in *Hound of Death; Witness and Other Stories*

Witness for the Prosecution—play and film based on above ss

Witness for the Prosecution and Other Stories—1948 ss collection

World's End—ss in *The Mysterious Mr. Quin*

Y

Yellow Iris—ss in *Regatta Mystery*

Yellow Jasmine Mystery—ss made over into novel chapter in *The Big Four*

APPENDIX B

Full-length Novels Alphabetised

All novels listed alphabetically under English (original) title. If you cannot find the title you are seeking, look it up in the general index (Appendix A). There you should find a cross reference from your title to the original title of the novel. If you look up the novel under its original title, you will find full particulars.

Full-length Novels

A.B.C. Murders, The (1935—Poirot). The classic inspired by Father Brown's remark, "Where to hide a tree but in a forest?" A murderer announces, in advance, by means of letters to Poirot, the site of the crimes he plans to commit in alphabetical order. Film version (1966) starring Tony Randall under the title "The Alphabet Murders." *Pocket Book.*

After the Funeral (1953—Poirot)—American title *Funerals Are Fatal* (including *Pocket Book* paperback). The Abernethie deaths cause Poirot some vexation, for people and pictures are not what they seem. Film version, with Miss Marple substituted for Poirot, under the title "Murder at the Gallop," starring Margaret Rutherford. Fontana (English) paperback, under the title *Murder at the Gallop, fb 912.*∗

∗ English paperback editions of Agatha Christie are published by Fontana Books or by Pan Books Limited.

Appointment with Death (1938—Poirot). Mrs. Boynton, an elderly American harridan, terrorises her husband's four children as the entourage travels through the Holy Land. Dramatised (1945) by the author into a play of the same name. A *Dell* paperback. Also available in Dodd, Mead omnibus volume entitled *Make Mine Murder* (q.v.).

At Bertram's Hotel (1965—Miss Marple). Miss Marple, visiting a quaint hotel of her childhood which has kept its Edwardian charm, is thrown once again into the midst of murder. She concludes, reluctantly, that you can't go back and relive the past. *Pocket Book.*

Big Four, The (1927—Poirot). Originally a set of short stories, but published in novel form. Hastings and Poirot track down a four-member cartel which plans world domination. Contains Hercule's short-lived brother Achille, also the famous chess-problem story. *Dell* paperback.

Body in the Library, The (1942—Miss Marple). Agatha Christie considers this first chapter her best beginning. "So," she says, "an elderly crippled man became the pivot of the story. Colonel and Mrs. Bantry, those old cronies of my Miss Marple, had just the right kind of library." *Pocket Book.*

Cards on the Table (1936—Poirot). Poirot is invited to a party where, he is told, there will be four murderers and four detectives. Poirot solves the subsequent murder of his host by analysing the bridge hands of the "murderers" involved. A *Dell* paperback. Also in Dodd, Mead omnibus volume, *Surprise Endings,* q.v.

Caribbean Mystery, A (1964—Miss Marple). Vacationing, on the island of St Honoré, Miss Marple keeps her eyes and ears on Major Palgrave as he is telling one of his old hunting stories. Possibly, if you keep your eye on what he does, you will see what he saw, and what led to his murder. *Pocket Book.*

Cat Among the Pigeons (1959—Poirot). Murder at Meadowbank, a girls' boarding school in England. Jewels in a tennis racquet culminate a month of murder and kidnapping. *Pocket Book.*

Clocks, The (1963—Poirot). "The more outré the crime, the more obvious the solution," said Poe, and Poirot muses on the minds of famous fictional detectives. Colin Lamb appears, but won't reveal his father's real name, for fear of being accused of capitalising on the old man's name. "I rather think," confides Mrs. Christie, however, with a twinkle in her eye, "that he is Superintendent Battle's son." Two plots very ingeniously interwoven. *Pocket Book.*

Crooked House (1949). Says Mrs. Christie, "This book is one of my own special favourites. I saved it up for years, working it out. . . . I don't know what put the Leonides family into my head—they just came. Then, like Topsy, 'they growed.' I feel that I myself was only their scribe." The title comes from the last line of the nursery rhyme. *Pocket Book.*

Dead Man's Folly (1956—Poirot). That famous lady detective writer, Ariadne Oliver, invites Poirot to a house-party where a "murder-hunt" will occur. But the local girl guide who plays the body ends up killed. Poirot finds out Who is Who. *Pocket Book.*

Death Comes as the End (1945). Spurred on by an Egyptologist-friend of her husband's, Mrs. Christie set a murder in Egypt, during the Middle Kingdom, 3000 years ago, showing clearly that human nature does not change, particularly where love and hate are concerned. She acknowledged, afterwards, that "practically all the questions, especially the most trivial, required a lot of research to answer." *Pocket Book.*

Death in the Clouds (1935—Poirot)—American title *Death in the Air. A Popular Library paperback.* Murder aboard an airplane provides Poirot with a closed-room puzzle that is probably one of the "closest" crimes he has solved. *Pan* (English) paperback X317.

Death on the Nile (1937—Poirot). Says Mrs. Christie about this work, "I think, myself, that the book is one of the best of my 'foreign travel' ones. I think the central situation is intriguing and has dramatic possibilities, and the three characters Simon, Linnet, and Jacqueline seem to me to be real and alive." A Bantam paperback. Dramatised in 1946

by the author into a play titled "Murder on the Nile."
Neither novel nor play has any connexion with the short
story titled "Death on the Nile." In Dodd, Mead omnibus
volume entitled *Perilous Journeys of Hercule Poirot,* q.v.

Destination Unknown (1954)—American title *So Many Steps to
Death.* The defection of an atomic scientist to a country
behind the Iron Curtain and the desire of a young redhead
to commit suicide combine in Casablanca. *Pocket Book,* under American title.

Dumb Witness (1937—Poirot)—American title *Poirot Loses a
Client.* Other titles: *Mystery at Littlegreen House, Murder
at Littlegreen House.* One of the last books in which Hastings appears. Poirot receives a letter from Miss Arundell,
who fears for her life—two months after her death. Yet
Poirot tracks down the murderer, who used Mrs. Christie's
favourite means of disposal—poison. *Dell* paperback, under
Poirot Loses a Client.

Evil Under the Sun (1941—Poirot). Poirot, at a seaside resort
in Devon, comes upon a love triangle with more angles
than meet the eye. Suspect even the victim. *Pocket Book.*

Five Little Pigs (1943—Poirot)—American title *Murder in
Retrospect.* A *Dell* paperback. Poirot investigates a murder
sixteen years old—clears the victim's wife, and finds the real
culprit. Remember who overheard which conversations.
Dramatised by the author (1960) into play entitled "Go
Back for Murder." In Dodd, Mead omnibus volume *Murder Preferred.* q.v.

4:50 from Paddington (1957—Miss Marple)—American titles
What Mrs. McGillicuddy Saw! and *Murder She Said.* Miss
Marple's friend Mrs. McGillicuddy sees a murder committed
before her eyes as a train passes her. She and Miss Marple,
together with Lucy Eylesbarrow, track down the murderer
and the victim. Film version starring Margaret Rutherford
under title "Murder She Said." *Pocket Books* paperback,
also under title *Murder She Said.*

Hercule Poirot's Christmas (1938—Poirot)—American titles
Murder for Christmas and *A Holiday for Murder.* Simeon
Lee, a nasty old millionaire, invites all his sons and daugh-

ters-in-law to visit him for Christmas, in order to be able
to torment them. Not surprisingly, one of the group does
what most of us would like to do at family gatherings, and
commits murder. Poirot, visiting nearby, discovers who and
why. *Bantam* paperback, under title *A Holiday for Murder*.

Hickory, Dickory, Dock (1955—Poirot)—American title *Hickory, Dickory, Death*. Miss Lemon, that secretary who has
served both Parker Pyne and M. Poirot, does the unthinkable—she makes three errors in typing a letter. It turns out
that she and her sister (who runs an international student
boarding house) can lead Poirot to poisoning. The nursery
rhyme figures tantalisingly in the tale. A *Pocket Book* under the American title.

Hollow, The (1946—Poirot)—American title *Murder After
Hours*. Poirot is vexed in this murder case, for he is working against a creative mind, not a destructive one. Apparently the doctor's wife is guilty, but it is the Trojan
horse that finally yields up the secret. Lady Angkatell
and her family all seem to know the secret, but politely try
to keep from discovering it. *Dell* paperback, under title
Murder After Hours. Dramatised by the author (1951) into
play entitled "The Hollow."

Lord Edgware Dies (1933—Poirot)—American title: *Thirteen
at Dinner*. A *Dell* paperback. One of the famous early
Christie books. Lady Edgware can apparently be in two
places at once, but it is talk of Paris which gives the clue
away. Compare this book with *The Mirror Crack'd from
Side to Side* (Miss Marple—1962) to see how the two sleuths
tackle essentially the same problem. *Fontana* (English)
paperback.

Man in the Brown Suit, The (1924). The smell of mothballs
and the electrocution of a man in a tube station in London
start Anne Beddingfield off on an adventure that ends in
Africa. This book and *The Secret Adversary* make an interesting pair, for in both cases you have all the clues you
need to guess the identity of the super-criminal. A sharp-eyed
and quick-witted Christie fan should be fooled in one case,
but not in both. However, many have been. . . . *Dell*.

Mirror Crack'd from Side to Side, The (1962—Miss Marple).

An American movie actress looks above her head at a party and is horrified by what she sees. After several murders, Miss Marple discovers why. Compare with *Lord Edgware Dies*. *Pocket Book*—American title shortened to *The Mirror Crack'd*.

Moving Finger, The (1943—Miss Marple). Flyer Jerry Burton comes to a quiet village with his sister to recover from a plane crash. But then the anonymous letters start arriving, accusing all sorts of people of all sorts of things. Murder ensues before Miss Marple has a chance to solve the problem. *Dell* paperback.

Mrs. McGinty's Dead (1952—Poirot). Poirot muses upon the question "What's in a name?" and comes up with the reason why Mrs. McGinty, a charwoman, should have been murdered after she recognised a photograph. Film version with Miss Marple substituted for Poirot, starring Margaret Rutherford, entitled "Murder Most Foul." *Pocket Book*.

Murder at the Vicarage (1930—Miss Marple). This is Miss Marple's first appearance in novel form. The Vicar, Len Clement, is a priceless character sketch. Some editions (i.e., first American edition) have a map of that famous hamlet, St. Mary Mead, as it looked in the early 1930's. Don't miss the description of Raymond West in his younger literary days. A *Dell* paperback. Dramatised by Moie Charles and Barbara Toy (1950) into play of same name. *Fontana* (English) paperback.

Murder in Mesopotamia (1936—Poirot). Archaeology, spying, and murder in Iraq, inspired by the Mallowans' travels in that part of the world. *Dell*.

Murder Is Announced, A (1950—Miss Marple). Agatha Christie's fiftieth book, the publication of which occasioned Margery Allingham's article in the *New York Times* book review. Watch your spelling very carefully. It is in this book that Miss Marple takes up ventriloquism. *Pocket Book*.

Murder Is Easy (1939)—American title *Easy to Kill*. Luke Fitzwilliam, on the train to London, sits next a lady who is en route to Scotland Yard to voice suspicions about some strange deaths in her town. But Fitzwilliam reads next day that she was run down before she ever got there. He and

Superintendent Battle finally run the murderer to ground. *Pocket Book,* under title *Easy to Kill.*

Murder of Roger Ackroyd, The (1926—Poirot). *The* classic Christie, whose surprise ending still causes endless debate. A must for every library. Says Mrs. Christie, "Some readers have cried indignantly, 'Cheating!'—an accusation that I have had pleasure in refuting by calling attention to various turns of phrasing and careful wording." Dramatised by Michael Morton (1928) into play entitled "Alibi." *Pocket Book.*

Murder on the Links (1923—Poirot). Poirot and Hastings arrive too late to save their employer, who has been murdered on his own golf links. Hastings is hopelessly in love at the end of this one. Begins and ends with the " 'Hell!' said the duchess" anecdote. *Dell.*

Murder on the Orient Express (1934—Poirot)—American title: *Murder in the Calais Coach.* A *Pocket Book.* One of the few cases in which Poirot lets murder go unpunished. One critic uncharitably remarked that the plot was so simple only a half-wit could have thought it up. One presumes that he failed to see through it. Incidentally, Poirot received a souvenir from this experience which he refers to in later novels. *Fontana* (English) paperback.

Mysterious Affair at Styles, The (1920—Poirot). Sutherland Scott called this book "one of the finest firsts ever written." Created while Sherlock Holmes was still very much alive, this book introduces Poirot to the world and marks the beginning of Mrs. Christie's literary career. A particularly vivid portrait of an England suffering from the economies of World War I—only three gardeners as opposed to the pre-war five! The young Inspector Japp also makes an appearance, as does Hastings. *Bantam.*

Mystery of the Blue Train (1928—Poirot). Murder on the luxury boat-train from London to the Riviera. An especially interesting account of upper-class travel and vacationing in the 1920's. *Pocket Book.* In Dodd, Mead omnibus volume *Perilous Journeys of Hercule Poirot,* q.v.

N or M? (1941—Tommy and Tuppence Beresford). The young adventurers from *The Secret Adversary* and *Partners in*

Crime re-appear, and prove to their children that the older generation still know a thing or two—in fact, enough to catch German agents in England. One of Mrs. Christie's best spy-adventure stories. *Dell* paperback, under title *N or M?*

One, Two, Buckle My Shoe (1940—Poirot)—American title *The Patriotic Murders*. The one which begins with Hercule Poirot in his dentist's office—just before the dentist is murdered. The nursery rhyme is used throughout. *Dell* paperback, under title *An Overdose of Death*.

Ordeal by Innocence (1958). A doctor returning from Antarctica is saddened to find that he could have prevented the wrong man from being convicted of murder if he had read the papers before he had left on the expedition. But for some reason everyone involved would rather not have the case pursued further. *Pocket Book.*

Pale Horse, The (1961). Is it possible to murder by telepathy? Mrs. Ariadne Oliver tells you the answer, if you listen at the right time. *Pocket Book.*

Peril at End House (1932—Poirot). Poirot is almost bested by the fair sex, whose tricks are anything but fair in this instance. Another seaside resort, with a girl whose life appears to be in very real danger. Watch the falling pictures. Dramatised by Arnold Ridley (1940) into play of same title. *Pocket Book.*

Pocket Full of Rye, A (1953—Miss Marple). Another mystery in which the murderer has a fascination for following a nursery rhyme. The "King"—Rex Fortescue—was in his counting-house, counting out his money when he died. Miss Marple arrives in time to ask about the four and twenty blackbirds. *Pocket Book.*

Sad Cypress (1940—Poirot). Elinor Carlisle is accused of poisoning Mary Gerrard, and the book opens as the former is on trial. Poirot uncovers the true identity of the major characters, and the skilful plot which very nearly succeeded. Mrs. Christie knows not only poisons, but their antidotes as well. *Dell.*

Secret Adversary, The (1922—Tommy and Tuppence Beresford). The first appearance of the dynamic couple. Compare this tale of the discovery of a master criminal with *The Man in the Brown Suit*. *Pan* (English) paperback X265. *Bantam* paperback.

Secret of Chimneys, The (1925). Anthony Cade and Superintendent Battle in a clash of wits. The plot and characters are quite complicated and involved, but the facts are in front of the reader. *Dell.*

Seven Dials Mystery, The (1929). Chimneys, the estate used for murder in the above mystery, figures again as its rightful owner, the Marquis of Caterham, takes it over once more. His daughter, the sprightly Lady Eileen ("Bundle"), almost drives her father to death at speeds he cannot endure, but ends up with the right man and and the criminal is unmasked. "Seven Dials" here refers to the secret organisation which apparently took its name from the neighborhood in London's district of the same name. A *Bantam* paperback.

Sittaford Mystery (1931)—American title *Murder at Hazelmoor*. Another session at séance, with a murder forecast. Sure enough, the murder materialises, in spite of the weather. An amusing portrait of a retired Army officer who dislikes young people—and for good reason. *Dell* paperback, under the title *Murder at Hazlemoor*.

Sparkling Cyanide (1945)—American title, *Remembered Death*. Colonel Race reappears for the first time since *The Man in the Brown Suit* (1924). For good reason was he absent from both birthday parties at which a murder was committed by putting cyanide in champagne. *Pocket Book,* under title *Remembered Death*. Expanded form of ss "Yellow Iris."

Taken at the Flood (1948—Poirot)—American title, *There Is a Tide*. A rich young widow named Rosaleen has to meet her in-laws, and, as might be suspected, a murder or two ensue. The tide, it appears, was not taken soon enough. But Poirot undoes all of the mysteries which surround the situation. *Dell* paperback.

Ten Little Niggers (1939)—American titles *Ten Little Indians; And Then There Were None; The Nursery Rhyme Murders*. Perhaps Mrs. Christie's most ingenious plot. If you have only seen one of the stage or screen versions, you will be even more amazed at the ingenuity of the original ending. Dramatised by the author (1943). Two film versions—first (1945) with Barry Fitzgerald and Walter Huston, released in USA with title "And Then There Were None." Second version (1965) with Wilfred Hyde-White and Stanley Holloway with title "Ten Little Indians." *Pocket Book,* under titles *And Then There Were None* and *Ten Little Indians.*

They Came to Baghdad (1951). Archaeology, love, and British Intelligence in Baghdad in a plot inspired by the Mallowans' expeditions to that part of the world. *Dell.*

They Do It with Mirrors (1952—Miss Marple)—American title *Murder with Mirrors.* A *Pocket Book.* Mrs. van Rydock worried about her sister Carrie Louise, turns to Miss Marple, who not only finds out what's troubling her, but also solves murder as well. *Fontana* (English) paperback.

Third Girl (1966—Poirot). Mrs. Ariadne Oliver reappears, and is coshed on the head. Poirot solves a mystery in "swinging" London, after he is challenged as being "too old." And many favourite Christie devices are used, to the confusion even of the experienced reader. *Pocket Book.*

Three-Act Tragedy (1935—Poirot)—American title *Murder in Three Acts.* The theatre and its people inspire this rehearsal for murder, but, as the foreword modestly suggests, with "Illumination by Hercule Poirot." A good chance that even Poirot might have been killed. Compare with *The A.B.C. Murders. Popular Library* paperback, under title *Murder in Three Acts.*

Towards Zero (1944)—American title *Come and Be Hanged.* Superintendent Battle wishes that Poirot were there, for a fireplace ornament is out of order. Yet a person's plan for murder almost comes off, except that a former suicide happens to walk up the street at the right time. Proving the matter is more difficult, however, even after one decides which is the murder that inspired the whole plot. *Pocket Book.* Dramatised by Agatha Christie and Gerald Verner (1956) into play entitled "Towards Zero."

Why Didn't They Ask Evans? (1934)—American title *The Boomerang Clue.* Bobby Jones finds a mortally-injured man who has fallen over a cliff. Jones notices a snapshot in the man's pocket, and is glad to pursue the problem when it appears that someone wishes that Jones and his girl friend were out of the way. *Dell* paperback, under title *The Boomerang Clue.*

Short Story Collections Alphabetised

In general, look up a short story title in Appendix A (general title index) before looking it up here, as Appendix A will tell you which collection the story appears in. As the reader will perceive from looking at the contents of these collections, it is impossible to collect the complete Christie without having some duplication, as the English and American collections have seldom included the same stories.

Adventure of the Christmas Pudding—1960 ss collection, England only. *Fontana* (English) paperback fb 896

Adventure of the Christmas Pudding—Poirot. Expanded form of "The Theft of the Royal Ruby"

Mystery of the Spanish Chest—Poirot. Expanded form of "The Mystery of the Baghdad Chest"

Under Dog—Poirot

Four and Twenty Blackbirds—Poirot

The Dream—Poirot

Greenshaw's Folly—Miss Marple

Dead Man's Mirror—1937 ss collection, America only. *Murder in the Mews* contains all that this collection does, plus "The Incredible Theft."

Dead Man's Mirror—Poirot. Expanded from ss "Second Gong"

Murder in the Mews—Poirot

Triangle at Rhodes—Poirot

Double Sin and Other Stories—1961 ss collection, America only. *Pocket Book* #6144

Double Sin—Poirot

Wasps' Nest—Poirot

Theft of the Royal Ruby—Poirot—see *Adventures of the Christmas Pudding*

Dressmaker's Doll

Greenshaw's Folly—Miss Marple

Double Clue—Poirot

Last Séance—see *Hound of Death*

Sanctuary—Miss Marple

Hound of Death—1933 ss collection, England only. *Fontana* (English) paperback fb 970

Hound of Death

Red Signal

Fourth Man

Gypsy

Lamp

Wireless (another title: Where There's a Will)

Witness for the Prosecution

Mystery of the Blue Jar

Strange Case of Sir Arthur Carmichael

Call of Wings

Last Séance

S O S

Labours of Hercules—1947 ss collection, all Poirot. *Dell* paperback #4620

How It All Came About—Foreword

Nemean Lion

Lernean Hydra

Arcadian Deer

Eurymanthian Boar

Augean Stables

Stymphalean Birds

Cretan Bull

Horses of Diomedes

Girdle of Hippolyta

Flock of Geryon

Apples of the Hesperides

Capture of Cerberus

Listerdale Mystery—1934 ss collection, England only. *Fontana*
(English) paperback fb 493

Listerdale Mystery

Philomel Cottage

Girl in the Train

Sing a Song of Sixpence

Manhood of Edward Robinson

Accident

Jane in Search of a Job

A Fruitful Sunday

Mr. Eastwood's Adventure (American title Mystery of the
Spanish Shawl)

Golden Ball

Rajah's Emerald

Swan Song

Murder in the Mews—1937 ss collection, all Poirot, England
only. *Fontana* (English) paperback fb 984

Murder in the Mews

Incredible Theft

Dead Man's Mirror. Expanded from ss "Second Gong"

Triangle at Rhodes

Mysterious Mr. Quin—1930 ss collection. Another title *The
Passing of Mr. Quin. Dell* paperback #6246

Coming of Mr. Quin

Shadow on the Glass

At the Bells and Motley

Sign in the Sky

Soul of the Croupier

World's End

Voice in the Dark

Face of Helen

Dead Harlequin

Bird with the Broken Wing

Man from the Sea

Harlequin's Lane

Parker Pyne Investigates—1934 ss collection, all Pyne. *Fontana*
(English) paperback 667

Case of the Middle-Aged Wife

Case of the Discontented Soldier

Case of the Distressed Lady

Case of the Discontented Husband
Case of the City Clerk
Case of the Rich Woman
Have You Got Everything You Want?
The Gate of Baghdad
The House at Shiraz
The Pearl of Price
Death on the Nile (no relation to novel of same name)
Oracle at Delphi

Partners in Crime—1929 ss collection, with Tommy and Tuppence Beresford. *Dell* paperback #6848
A Fairy in the Flat
A Pot of Tea
The Affair of the Pink Pearl
The Affair of the Sinister Stranger
Finessing the King
The Gentleman Dressed in Newspaper
The Case of the Missing Lady
Blindman's Buff
The Man in the Mist
The Crackler
The Sunningdale Mystery
The House of Lurking Death
The Unbreakable Alibi
The Clergyman's Daughter
The Red House
The Ambassador's Boots
The Man Who Was Number 16 (the famous satire on Poirot and his methods)

Poirot Investigates—1924 ss collection, all Poirot. *Bantam* paperback #J2604
Adventure of the Western Star
Tragedy at Marsdon Manor
Adventure of the Cheap Flat
Mystery of Hunter's Lodge
Million Dollar (Bond) Bank Robbery
Adventure of the Egyptian Tomb
Jewel Robbery at the Grand Metropolitan
Kidnapped Prime Minister
Disappearance of Mr. Davenheim
Adventure of the Italian Nobleman

Case of the Missing Will

Veiled Lady (not published in the English collection of this same name)

Lost Mine (not published in the English collection of this same name)

Chocolate Box (not published in the English collection of this same name)

Regatta Mystery—1939 ss collection, America only *Dell* paperback #7336

Regatta Mystery—Pyne

Mystery of the Baghdad Chest—Poirot, (See "Mystery of the Spanish Chest" in *Adventure of the Christmas Pudding*.)

How Does Your Garden Grow?—Poirot

Problem at Pollensa Bay—Pyne

Yellow Iris—Poirot. Expanded into novel *Sparkling Cyanide*

Miss Marple Tells a Story—Miss Marple

The Dream—Poirot

In a Glass Darkly

Problem at Sea—Poirot

Surprise! Surprise!—ss collection, America only (1965), containing stories previously published in other collections —no new material

13 Clues for Miss Marple—ss collection, America only (1966), containing stories previously published in other collections—no new material

13 for Luck—ss collecton, America only (1961), containing stories previously published in other collections—no new material

Thirteen Problems—1932 ss collection, all Miss Marple. American title *The Tuesday Club Murders, Dell* paperback #9136

Tuesday Night Club

Idol House of Astarte

Ingots of Gold

The Bloodstained Pavement

Motive versus Opportunity

Thumb Mark of St. Peter

Blue Geranium

Companion

Four Suspects

Christmas Tragedy

Herb of Death

Affair at the Bungalow

Death by Drowning

Three Blind Mice and Other Stories—1950 ss collection America only. Also called *The Mousetrap and Other Stories*. *Dell* paperback #D354

Three Blind Mice

Strange Jest

Tape-Measure Murder. Another title "Case of the Retired Jeweller"

Case of the Perfect Maid

Case of the Caretaker

The Third Floor Flat

Adventure of Johnny Waverly

Four and Twenty Blackbirds

Love Detectives

Under Dog and Other Stories—1952 ss collection all Poirot, America only. *Dell* paperback #9228

Under Dog

Plymouth Express

Affair at the Victory Ball

Market Basing Mystery

Lemesurier Inheritance

Cornish Mystery

King of Clubs

Submarine Plans

Adventure of the Clapham Cook

Witness for the Prosecution and Other Stories—1948 ss collection, America only. *Dell* paperback #9619

Witness for the Prosecution

Red Signal

Fourth Man

S O S

Where There's a Will (English title Wireless)

Mystery of the Blue Jar

Philomel Cottage

Accident

The Second Gong—Poirot. Expanded into ss "Dead Man's Mirror"

Books and Stories Made into Plays

Samuel French publish all of Agatha Christie's plays. Apply to:

> Samuel French, Ltd.
> 26, Southampton Street, Strand
> London, England

or:

> Samuel French, Inc.
> 25 West 45th Street
> New York, New York 10036

Alibi (1928) from novel *Murder of Roger Ackroyd;* dramatised by Michael Morton

Appointment with Death (1945) from novel of same name; dramatised by the author

Black Coffee (1934) original play

Go Back for Murder (1960) from novel *Five Little Pigs;* dramatised by the author

Hollow, The (1951) from novel of same name; dramatised by the author

Love from a Stranger (1936) from ss Philomel Cottage; dramatised by Agatha Christie and Frank Vosper

Mousetrap, The (1952) from radio play for eightieth birthday Queen Mary, and based on ss *Three Blind Mice* (published

America only, in ss coll. of same name), dramatised by the author

Murder at the Vicarage (1950) from novel of same name; dramatised by Moie Charles and Barbara Toy

Murder on the Nile (1946) from novel (not short story) *Death on the Nile;* dramatised by the author

Peril at End House (1940) from novel of same name; dramatised by Arnold Ridley

Rule of Three (1962) three one-act original plays

> a. Afternoon at the Seaside
> b. Patient
> c. Rats

Spider's Web (1954) original play

Ten Little Niggers (1943) from novel of same name; dramatised (and with new ending) by the author. Also known as *Ten Little Indians; And Then There Were None*

Towards Zero (1956) from novel of same name; dramatised by the author and Gerald Verner

Unexpected Guest (1958) original play

Verdict (1958) original play

Witness for the Prosecution (1953) based on ss of same name; dramatised by the author

APPENDIX E

Books and Stories Made into Films

Films listed by title, with cross reference to the novels, plays, and short stories from which the plots were drawn.

Alphabet Murders—from novel *The A.B.C. Murders*, with Tony Randall as Hercule Poirot

Black Coffee—from original play

Love from a Stranger—from play of same name, based on ss "Philomel Cottage."
First version: with Basil Rathbone, Madeleine Carroll
Second version: with John Hodiak, Sylvia Sidney

Murder at the Gallop—from novel *After the Funeral*, with Margaret Rutherford as Miss Marple substituted for Hercule Poirot

Murder Most Foul—from novel *Mrs. McGinty's Dead*, with Margaret Rutherford as Miss Marple substituted for Hercule Poirot

Murder She Said—from novel *4:50 from Paddington*, with Margaret Rutherford as Miss Marple

Spider's Web—from original play of same name, starring Margaret Lockwood

Ten Little Indians (1965)—film version with Stanley Holloway, Fabian *et al.*, based on play "Ten Little Niggers"

Ten Little Niggers (1945) film version of play of same name with Barry Fitzgerald, Walter Huston, Louis Haywood. Released in America as "And Then There Were None"

Witness for the Prosecution—from play of same name, with Charles Laughton, Elsa Lanchester, Marlene Dietrich

Note: *Murder Ahoy,* with Margaret Rutherford as Miss Marple, was based on a script written by MGM, not by Agatha Christie. It was a doubtful artistic success.

Titles Not Published in America and Titles Not Published in England, as of 1967

Short stories not published in America

Adventure of the Christmas Pudding (in ss coll. of same name)

Call of Wings (in ss coll. *Hound of Death*)

Fruitful Sunday (in ss coll. *Listerdale Mystery*)

Girl in the Train (in ss coll. *Listerdale Mystery*)

Golden Ball (in ss coll. *Listerdale Mystery*)

Gypsy (in ss coll. *Hound of Death*)

Hound of Death (in ss coll. of same name)

Incredible Theft (in ss coll. *Murder in the Mews*)

Jane in Search of a Job (in ss coll. *Listerdale Mystery*)

Lamp (in ss coll. *Hound of Death*)

Listerdale Mystery (in ss coll. of same name)

Manhood of Edward Robinson (in ss coll. *Listerdale Mystery*)

Mystery of the Spanish Chest (in ss coll. *Adventure of the Christmas Pudding*)

Rajah's Emerald (in ss coll. *Listerdale Mystery*)

Sing a Song of Sixpence (in ss coll. *Listerdale Mystery*)

Strange Case of Sir Arthur Carmichael (in ss coll. *Hound of Death*)

Swan Song (in ss coll. *Listerdale Mystery*)

Short stories not published in England

Adventure of Johnny Waverly—Poirot, also called The Kidnapping of Johnny Waverly (in ss coll. *Three Blind Mice*)

Adventure of the Clapham Cook (in ss coll. *The Under Dog*)

Adventure of the King of Clubs (in ss coll. *The Under Dog*)

Affair at the Victory Ball (in ss coll. *The Under Dog*)

Case of the Caretaker (in ss coll. *Three Blind Mice*)

Case of the Perfect Maid—also called Maid Who Disappeared (in ss coll. *Three Blind Mice*)

Chocolate Box (in American ss coll. *Poirot Investigates*, but not in English coll. of same title)

Cornish Mystery (in ss coll. *The Under Dog*)

Lemesurier Inheritance (in ss coll. *The Under Dog*)

Lost Mine (in American ss coll. *Poirot Investigates*, but not in English coll. of same title)

Love Detectives (in ss coll. *Three Blind Mice*)

Market Basing Mystery (in ss coll. *The Under Dog*)

Mystery of the Plymouth Express (in ss coll. *The Under Dog*)

Strange Jest—Miss Marple, also called Case of the Buried Treasure (in ss coll. *Three Blind Mice*)

Submarine Plans (in ss coll. *The Under Dog*)

Tape-Measure Murder—also called Case of the Retired Jeweller (in ss coll. *Three Blind Mice*)

Three Blind Mice (ss in coll. of same name)

Third Floor Flat (in ss coll. *Three Blind Mice*)

Veiled Lady (in American ss coll. *Poirot Investigates*, but not in English coll. of same title)

The Nursery Rhymes Used by Agatha Christie in Her Mystery Novels and Short Stories

All harmonisations are by the author.

I. Sing a Song of Sixpence. Used in "Four and Twenty Blackbirds," "Sing a song of Sixpence," and *A Pocket Full of Rye*.

Sing a song of six - pence, A pock - et full of rye.

Four and twen-ty black-birds baked in a pie. When the pie was o - pened, the

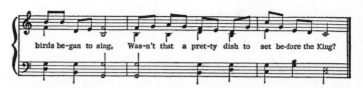

birds be-gan to sing, Was-n't that a pret-ty dish to set be-fore the King?

The king was in his counting house, counting out his money,
The queen was in her parlour, eating bread and honey,
The maid was in the garden, hanging out the clothes,
When along came a blackbird, and snipped off her nose!

II. Hickory, Dickory, Dock. Used in novel of same name.

Hick-or-y, dick-or-y dock!___ The mouse ran up___ the clock.___ The

clock struck one, the mouse ran down, Hick-or-y, dick-or-y dock!

III. One, Two, Buckle My Shoe. Used in novel of same name (American title: *The Patriotic Murders*).

IV. There Was a Crooked Man. Used in novel *Crooked House.*

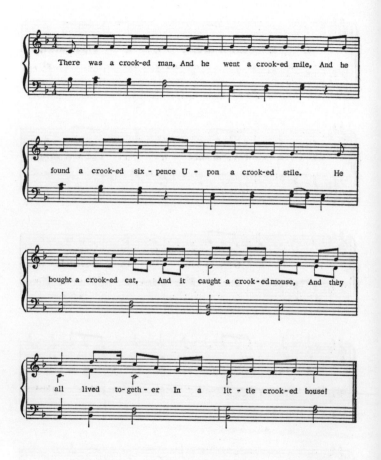

V. Three Blind Mice. Used in short story "Three Blind Mice," and in radio and stage play adaptation "The Mousetrap."

VI. Five Little Pigs. Mrs. Christie says that she did not know that this rhyme had a tune. The tune quoted below is from *The Oxford Nursery Song Book,* collected and arranged by Percy Buck [London, no date].

VII. The American rhyme "Ten Little Indians" (see text, p. 43) has no relationship to the English nursery rhyme "Ten Little Niggers," which Mrs. Christie used in the novel and play of the latter name. The American publishers substituted "Indians" for "Niggers" in the American publications to avoid any ill-feeling, as "nigger" as a colloquialism for "Negro" has a disparaging connotation in the States. Nevertheless, for those who desire a tune for the English rhyme, the American tune can be (and in film versions has been) adapted to fit the English rhyme, as shown below. The English rhyme has, apparently, never had a tune of its own.

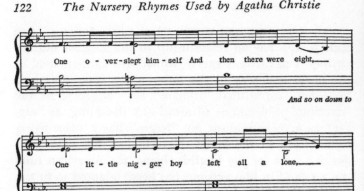

One   o - ver - slept him - self And   then   there were   eight,___

And so on down to

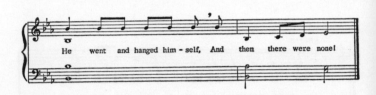

One   lit - tle   nig - ger   boy   left   all   a   lone,___

He   went   and hanged him - self, And   then   there were   none!

Bibliography

I. *Selected books on the history and writing of detective fiction*

1. Brean, Herbert (ed.), *Mystery Writer's Handbook,* Harper and Bros., New York, 1956. This book, a collection of essays by experts in the field, was published under the auspices of the Mystery Writers of America. It offers a fascinating behind-the-scenes account of what goes into the making of a detective story.
2. Gilbert, Michael (ed.), *Crime in Good Company,* Constable and Co., London, 1959. A British Companion volume to the above, published under the aegis of the Crime Club.
3. Haycraft, Howard, *Murder for Pleasure: The Life and Times of the Detective Story,* Appleton-Century, New York, 1941. Easily the most valuable book in the field, this volume is now unfortunately out of print, although still available in most metropolitan libraries. Mr. Haycraft says that a revised and up-to-date version will be the project of his retirement.

II. *Articles concerning Agatha Christie and her works*

1. Allingham, Margery, "Review of *A Murder Is Announced,*" front-cover essay and portrait in *The New York Times Book Review,* Sunday, 4 June 1950.

2. Dennis, Nigel, "Genteel Queen of Crime," *Life Magazine,* 14 May 1956.

3. Ramsey, G. C., "Perdurable Agatha," inside cover essay, *The New York Times* Book Review, Sunday, 21 November 1965.

4. Wyndham, Francis, "The Algebra of Agatha Christie," long interview and article in *London Sunday Times,* 27 February 1966. (Do not confuse with *The Times* of London.)

Short articles and pictures have not been listed here, as these four articles contain the majority of printed information about Agatha Christie.